CRESCENT KINGDOM

WOLVES OF CRESCENT CREEK

TESSA HALE

Bloom books

Published by Bloom Books, an imprint of Sourcebooks
1935 Brookdale RD, Naperville, IL 60563–2773
(630) 961-3900
sourcebooks.com

Previously self-published by Tessa Hale in 2025.

Cataloging-in-Publication data is on file with the Library of Congress.

Printed and bound in the United States of America.
LB 10 9 8 7 6 5 4 3 2 1

CRESCENT KINGDOM

Prologue

AGE NINE

Billy was sad. The teacher should've known just by looking at him. The way his head was bent, eyes focused on his hands. How he kept sniffling as he tried to keep the tears at bay. I'd learned to match the way people looked with their feelings. Because if I saw it before I felt it, I could sometimes make my shields stronger. But others, I wasn't fast enough.

Like now.

I'd been listening to Ms. Meyer talk about molecules, watching her draw them in a rainbow of colors on the whiteboard, and I hadn't seen it in time. Billy's sadness reached out with icy claws that tried to shred my chest. His hurt wanted to make a home in me, like I'd called to it in some way.

But my mom always said I couldn't let it in. That if I took on the world's pain, it would drown me. So, instead, I hid that I could feel it all.

We hid a lot, Mom and me. Like what our real names were and

who we were running from. Like the fact that I was half wolf and half caster. But most of all, that I couldn't just take on the world's feelings. I could heal them. Only, if I wasn't careful, that healing might make it so I never woke up again.

"Sarah," Ms. Meyer began, pulling me out of my thoughts—thoughts that weren't on her lessons at all. "Can you tell me what part of the atom electrons circle?"

I clenched my hands, my fingernails digging into my palms. The pain helped sometimes. If I could give myself that, it would distract me from the hurt hitting my shields.

But Billy was *so* sad. I didn't know why. I never got the *why*. I just knew the emotion. Sometimes, I could even name it before the person experiencing it did.

My head started to pound, like it always did when there was too much.

"Sarah?" Ms. Meyer asked, crossing to my desk. "Do you have a headache?"

My mom told her I got them, just like she told every teacher I'd ever had. If it got to be too much, I was supposed to ask to go to the nurse. But I'd already missed half a day this week. I didn't want to miss another.

I took a deep breath and focused on my heartbeat the way Mom had taught me. *"My Little Wren, listen to the song inside you. As long as you hear your voice, you'll always be able to come back to yourself."*

I heard the bah-bump, bah-bump, bah-bump of my heart. I listened to the song that was mine alone. And then the headache and pain in my chest began to ease.

Slowly, I opened my eyes. "The electrons circle the nuclei."

Ms. Meyer's lips twitched. "Sometimes, I need to close my eyes to think of the answer, too."

"Weirdo," Tara muttered from behind me and to the right.

My shields were already up, so I couldn't feel her anger and hate. I was used to that coming from her. Knew that I needed to guard and block because ugly feelings lived in her—not just toward others but for herself.

"Tara," Ms. Meyer warned. "We don't name-call in this class."

Tara just let out a huff of air in response.

"All right. Now, who can tell me—?" A knock cut off Ms. Meyer's words. "Come in."

The door opened tentatively, and Ms. Alder, the school receptionist, stood in the entryway. Her face was pale, and her eyes were wide. The image said fear, even with my shields up. She swallowed, her throat struggling with the action. "We need Sarah in the office." Her gaze darted to me and then quickly away again.

Sarah. That was me.

I had to remind myself of the name I was supposed to answer to. It changed so often—every time my mom decided we'd been someplace too long. It was hard to keep up with.

Ms. Meyer nodded, a hint of worry passing over her expression. "Of course. Go on."

Tara made a snickering sound behind me, but I ignored it. All I could think about was the look on Ms. Alder's face. Fear. Shock. Those weren't good emotions. They were the kind that clawed and sliced when I let them in.

I did what I always did. I searched for the reason. I was always trying to find the source. Because if I found that, maybe I could fix the feelings in another way—some way that wouldn't end with me never waking up.

My worn sneakers squeaked against the linoleum as I wove through the desks to get to Ms. Alder. The moment I reached her, she put a hand on my shoulder.

Comfort.

That was what she was trying to give to me. That knowledge only made me more nervous, my stomach doing dips and whirls. I swallowed, my tongue sticking to the roof of my mouth.

I glanced up at her as she guided me down the hall. "What's wrong?"

It took everything inside me to ask the question. Because I knew the answer could be bad. Had someone figured out one of my secrets? My supernatural side?

Mom had worked with me not only on my shields but also on how to hide my scent. The one that told other supes I was a hybrid. Because if they knew that, there was a chance they could tell my father.

The person we were running from.

Ms. Alder's jaw clenched so hard it looked like it might pop right out of the socket. "There are some people here who need to talk to you."

My stomach sank. I pictured humans in lab coats ready to drag me away. To experiment on me because I was different.

But as we rounded the corner, I saw something else. There were two police officers dressed in their typical blue uniforms, guns on their belts. And a woman in a suit who didn't quite fit right, her frizzy hair pulled back into a bun.

My stomach twisted again, my mind trying to put the pieces together. But before I could, that woman was striding forward. She had a gentle smile on her lips. "Hi, Sarah."

I didn't say a word. I couldn't.

The woman's smile wavered a bit. "Why don't we sit down?"

Ms. Alder's hand left my shoulder, replaced by the woman's as she guided me toward a bench outside the school office. The one you sat on when you were in trouble and waiting to see the principal. I'd never sat on it before.

As I lowered myself to the seat, the cold from the metal seeped through my jeans. I didn't look at the woman or the police officers speaking in hushed tones. I stared straight ahead, focused on the second graders' art projects lining the walls above the blue lockers. They were self-portraits. All different shapes and shades.

I tried to examine each and every one, to see the feelings in them. To understand them.

"Sarah." The woman cut into my thoughts. "I'm Maggie."

It was rare that adults gave me their first names. The use of hers now made me wary and on edge.

"I work with the police when children are involved in a case."

My gaze snapped to her, but still, no words came.

"I'm so sorry, Sarah, but your mom passed away this morning. She's with the angels."

A buzzing sound lit in my ears. It intensified with each second that passed, making my whole body vibrate with it. "No."

The word wasn't a whisper, but it wasn't a shout either. It was a demand. An order for this woman to tell me she was lying.

"I'm so sorry, Sarah."

I hated her saying the words over again. I hated her *sorries*. And I despised her use of a name that wasn't even mine.

"We were able to locate your father. We know you haven't seen him for some time, but he wants to be here for you now."

My spine snapped straight. Fear, thick and black, spread through me as I heard the soles of someone's dress shoes clicking on the linoleum.

No. No. No.

I barely remembered my father. Quick snapshots. I mostly remembered my mother's screams—the ones she let loose as he hit her.

But Mom showed me his photo once a month. That, along with pictures of his closest enforcers. All the people I needed to know so I could run if I saw them.

Only now, there was no option to run.

The man stepped into the artificial glow of one of the overhead lights. His sad look was just as fake as the light above him. I knew it just by looking, but I could feel it, too—the sliminess pushing against my shields.

Some part of me knew that if I let my protections down around this man, he would end me.

His dark, almost-black hair gleamed under the false light. It was perfectly arranged, just like the suit he wore. Too perfect. His dark eyes cut to me. "Fleur."

My stomach cramped. I hadn't heard that name in years. There were times I longed for it, craved to simply be myself again. But hearing it now? It didn't fit. Not anymore.

The man took a step closer. "Don't worry, Little Flower. I've got you now. And I'm going to take you home where you belong."

Icy dread coursed through me as my wolf pushed to the surface. She wanted to be free, to run fast and far from Bastian Boudreaux, my so-called father.

I should've listened to her.

CHAPTER ONE

Wren

FIFTEEN YEARS LATER

"Order up," Gary called across the pass-through window as he slid two plates piled high with burgers and fries onto the counter.

Arcane was one of only two bars in the small town of Crescent Creek, Colorado. And by small, I meant minuscule. The population sat right around sixteen hundred. It made sense when the location, nestled between the mountains, meant you could be locked in by snow for weeks at a time.

But I liked the isolated feeling. And the fact that you knew almost everyone. Just like every local knew that while Arcane was known for its booze, it also had the best burgers in town.

I grabbed the two plates, not bothering with a tray. "Thanks, Gar."

He simply gave me a chin lift in response, making the silver in his beard catch the light. Gary wasn't big on unnecessary conversation, and it was one of the things I loved most about the big, burly grandpa biker. He never prodded into my life.

It meant I didn't have to lie to him. I'd lived in at least a dozen different places in the eight years since I'd broken free of my father's reign of terror. I'd painted elaborate lies for my past. But they added weight every time I told them.

That could be part of the reason Crescent Creek had felt like home the minute I passed through its town limits. No one pushed. Maybe because those with secrets came here to hide.

There were a handful of supernaturals: a couple of fox shifters, a witch, and even a griffin. But with my scent shields in place, none even gave me a second look.

I tried telling myself that flying under the radar was good. Necessary. But at the thought, my wolf half pressed against my skin, letting loose a keening sound inside me. She missed the contact of her kind, the feeling of being in a pack. And she was getting more than restless at the lack of both.

Weaving through tables, I came to a stop at a two-top. Sliding the plates in front of the two out-of-towners, I glanced at their cups. "Need any refills?"

I felt the brown-haired one's eyes on me. His scrutiny slithered across my emotional shields like oily tentacles. "I think we're good. Any recs for a dinner spot tonight? We're in town on a fishing trip. Here for a couple of days."

I knew the game—the subtle tossing out that he was available for me to warm his bed for a night or two. It probably wouldn't have been a bad idea. He was decent-looking and could maybe satiate my wolf for a few weeks. Give her the touch she so desperately needed.

She bared her teeth in disagreement, scoffing at the idea of this human being even *close* to what she needed.

My shoulders slumped. So much for that idea. "I recommend Gino's, down the block. Great pizza and pasta."

The blond one leaned forward, his cologne invading my senses. "You could always meet us there."

I stepped back, trying to take a breath free of his sickly sweet scent. "Sorry, got plans. Flag me down if you need a refill or anything else."

My tip might suffer for my abrupt departure, but better that than breaking one of their arms because they put a hand on my ass. As I turned and walked away, the brown-haired one's voice caught my shifter hearing.

He let out a low whistle. "The body on that one."

"Fucking perfect," Blondie agreed. "It's too bad about her face."

Brown Hair chuckled. "I'd just take her from behind."

Anger coursed through me, the kind of rage I knew would take hours of sparring to work through. My fingers itched to move, to trace the scar running from the top of my forehead down my cheek.

Even now, all these years later, I could still feel the bite of the blade, the white-hot pain as I screamed and begged for mercy. But there was none. Never at the hands of Bastian Boudreaux.

It didn't matter how far I ran or how much time passed. I could still hear his voice in my head, taunting me in wakefulness and sleep.

"My daughter will not be a weakling. A submissive. She will be strong. *Even if I have to scar every inch of her body to make her so."*

CHAPTER TWO

Wren

"I CAN'T BELIEVE YOU'RE HEADING TO THE GYM AFTER working a double," Dina said, counting out cash behind the bar.

The manager of Arcane had worked in these kinds of places since she was eighteen. Now, at fifty-five, she wore that experience like armor. Locals rarely attempted to cross her, and if they did, they met the other end of her bat.

As she stood there in her black cowboy boots and salt-and-pepper hair woven into a braid that hung halfway down her back, I envied Dina. The way she was so sure of herself. How she knew exactly who she was and made no apologies for it.

I hoisted my duffel over my shoulder. "You know I'm always twitchy after a shift. Gotta work that out."

I'd only been in Crescent Creek for a little over a month, but Dina was observant. And her keen eye meant that even though to. Her gaze flicked to me, and then she went back to the money. "Give 'em hell."

I chuckled and headed for the back door. "Thanks, D. Get home safe."

As I slipped outside, I glanced at where my beat-up navy hatchback was parked. Not that anyone would want to steal it—its condition was too crappy. But I liked knowing it was still there. Just in case I needed to escape.

But I didn't need to use the vehicle daily, thanks to Dina renting me the studio apartment above the bar for a steal. I could walk everywhere I needed to go. It wasn't as if I went many places: the tiny grocery store a few blocks down, the woods behind the bar for a run in wolf form, and the gym.

Crescent Kingdom.

The name had called to me the moment I stopped in town, checking out what it had to offer and knowing I didn't have the cash to make it much farther. But Crescent Creek had been exactly what I needed. And the gym was, too.

As I pushed open the door, the familiar sound of gloved hands striking bags and mitts hit my ears. It created the most soothing symphony—the sound of home.

The place was humming, even at ten o'clock at night, largely because Crescent Kingdom's clientele worked long hours at other jobs. Fitting in fight training came after dinners with family or working double shifts at jobs like I did.

"Hey there, girlie. Thought you might be bailing tonight." Clyde ambled over in that stiff, limping walk he had—the gait of a fighter who'd reached his senior years.

I couldn't help the smile that pulled at my lips as I took in his grizzled face. "Never. Just took longer to close up tonight."

Clyde pinned me with a stare. "Rowdy customers?"

I'd never had a father. Not a real one, anyway—someone who cared about my well-being, happiness, and safety. I hadn't had grandparents either. As far as I knew, Bastian's parents were dead. And my mom never thought it would be safe for us to be in contact with hers.

But there was something about Clyde's gruff care and grandfatherly demeanor that made my chest ache in the most beautiful way.

"Nothing and no one I can't handle," I assured him.

Clyde chuckled. "I don't doubt that, girlie." He inclined his head toward a man in his late twenties, hitting a heavy bag. "Franco wants to spar if you're up for it. Getting ready for that bout in three weeks."

I watched the shirtless man connect with the bag, sweat glistening on his tan skin. He was fit, attractive, and moved with grace, but I felt nothing but respect for him. No tingling attraction or anything else. Maybe that part of me was broken.

"No problem," I agreed quickly. "Just need to warm up."

"I'll get the ring clear in thirty," Clyde said.

I gave him a quick nod and moved to the far wall, where I tucked my bag. Clyde had a small locker room for the handful of women who frequented the gym, but I didn't want my bag anywhere I couldn't see it, where it might be difficult to get to if I needed to bolt.

I'd learned the hard way to carry everything I needed with me: my current fake ID, along with at least two others, enough cash to get me through a couple of weeks, and a spare set of clothes.

Everything had to be ready so I could flee at a moment's notice and transform. I'd had every hair and eye color under the sun but was currently back to my natural dark brown with blue eyes that almost looked turquoise in certain light. There was only one thing I never changed.

My first name.

It was an homage to my mother—the only piece of her I still carried with me. Because each time I heard someone call my name, I heard my mom's voice in my head. *"My Little Wren, listen to the song inside you. As long as you hear your voice, you'll always be able to come back to yourself."*

I held tightly to that reminder, using my heart to ground me every time the pain got to be too much—other people's or mine.

Letting my duffel drop to the floor by the wall, I hopped onto a treadmill and turned up the speed to an easy jog. Many female fighters sparred in shorts and bra tops. I didn't have that option if I didn't want to answer questions about the scars riddling my body, so I opted for leggings and a long-sleeved workout shirt.

You could see a couple of the scars on my hands, but most people assumed I had been in a car accident of some sort. Because that made sense. No one would think my own father had inflicted the wounds.

I punched up the speed as the memories tried to take hold. The burn of my muscles always helped, as did my refusal to be a victim any longer.

If my father came for me again, he wouldn't find a trembling little girl.

"Wren," Clyde shouted over the music and the sounds of punches and kicks. "We're ready for you."

I slowed the treadmill's speed, easing back into a jog and then a walk. I didn't rush the process. That was how you ended up with a pulled or torn muscle, and I didn't have time for that.

Stopping the treadmill altogether, I hopped off and did a quick set of stretches. An exaggerated groan sounded to my right.

"Wren, you are *killing* me," Juan muttered. "When are you going to give in and marry me?"

My lips twitched as I glanced over at him from my forward bend. "When you can best me in the ring."

Franco chuckled and slapped Juan on the shoulder. "That's a no-chance-in-hell, my man."

Juan just grinned at him. "Never say never, just like the Biebs says."

Franco scowled. "Jesus."

I laughed. This sort of shit talking made me feel like one of the guys, even if I was sort of being hit on. I knew Juan wasn't serious, just like he wasn't serious about fighting. He did it for fun, to stay in shape, and to spend time with his friends.

If I really thought about it, he was probably the healthiest of us all. Because you often found people with demons in these sorts of gyms—those trying to beat them into submission. And it only worked for small snippets of time.

I straightened, testing my limbs to make sure they were loose and warm. "Let's do this."

Franco nodded, took a swig of water, and then tossed the bottle to Juan. "Don't hold back."

Clyde snickered. "Not sure you want to give her that kind of permission."

Warmth spread through me at Clyde's words and his belief in me. He had no idea what sort of gift that was.

I climbed into the practice ring, ducking between the ropes. Crescent Kingdom was a mixed martial arts gym on the whole, but people here generally specialized in boxing or jiujitsu. I wanted to learn it all. To know everything I could use to defeat my opponent.

Franco was training for a local MMA match a few towns over and was one of the fighters at the gym who could give me the best run for my money. He sauntered toward the center of the ring, holding out his knuckles covered by fingerless practice gloves.

Tugging mine on, I met him in the middle to touch fists.

"Ready?" Clyde called, backing away from the ring.

I liked the way Clyde coached. He moved around the ring, sometimes getting right up next to it for a closer view, other times backing off so he could see the full picture. He said it gave him perspective.

Franco lifted his chin in assent, and I did the same.

A whistle sounded in the distance.

Franco immediately rose to the tips of his toes, and we started the dance. Our movements came in testing jabs and kicks. Though we'd sparred countless times before, every day was different. You never knew what a person might be carrying with them in those moments.

Franco's fist shot out, trying to get my ribs. I blocked the worst of it, answering with a kick to his side, instantly rebuking myself. I should've gone for his legs, kicking them out from under him.

Too late now.

I moved quickly, darting in for an uppercut to Franco's jaw. His head snapped back, but he quickly righted himself. Neither of us was sparring at full strength. If we had been, that punch would have packed a hell of a lot more heat.

We dodged and wove, each landing the occasional hit. I had to admit, Franco was getting better.

"Stop holding back," he growled.

I should've known he'd realize what I was doing. He was too smart not to. I could never fight with my full shifter strength or speed in here, but I *was* holding back even the human part of me.

Giving Franco what he wanted, I lunged forward. Using my petite size, I ducked under his swing and swept his legs out from under him. Franco hit the mat with a loud thud as a collective series of *oooohs* sounded around us.

I moved in to pounce, to get him into an armbar or some other hold, but Franco was fast. He leapt to his feet before I got there, hands up by his face. We traded punches, and then the air shifted, something catching on it—a scent I hadn't smelled in weeks.

Wolf.

The shock was enough to have my guard slipping, my hands lowering. And then a fist connected hard with my jaw.

CHAPTER THREE

Kingston

THE MOMENT I STEPPED INTO THE GYM, I FINALLY FELT like I was home, unlike when I'd gotten to our pack lands or even our house. Crescent Kingdom had truly become my grounding place.

Six weeks away from it was way too fucking long. It didn't matter if it was for a mission to bring justice to countless souls. Or that we'd walked away with a whole new pile of cash lining our pockets. I hated being away for so long. Especially in the mountains of Siberia. It might be spring in Colorado, but it was the dead of winter there. And I was pretty sure the cold still lived in my bones.

The sound of gloves hitting bags was less than I would've expected given the number of vehicles in the parking lot. But the moment I scanned the room, I saw why.

She was captivating.

Everything in me stilled as I took in the female. My wolf

instantly rose, pressing against my skin, dying to break free. I took in a deep breath, letting her scent fill my lungs.

Human.

But somehow...different.

That second thought had my wolf going on high alert. There was something about it. A wrongness.

Was she sick? Injured?

As I watched the woman circle the ring, I knew neither of those could be true. She moved like a ballerina, but her hits had the force of someone five times her size. Franco was one of our top human fighters, and she was giving him a run for his money.

I took a few steps deeper into the gym, coming to stand next to my manager, Clyde. "Who is she?"

His gaze flicked to me for a beat before returning to the ring. "Gets in an hour ago, and he's already back at work."

"You know I can't stay away."

Clyde chuckled. "You know what they say about all work and no play."

"This is my play." That much was true. Creating a safe space for people to learn how to protect themselves and work through the worst things they'd been through had given me a purpose in my darkest hour.

Clyde simply scoffed.

"So," I pressed, feeling my wolf's impatience. My human half felt the emotion, too, but my wolf was the part of me I needed to worry about.

One corner of Clyde's mouth kicked up. "Got to town about a month ago. Name's Wren. I have to admit, I didn't think a little thing like her should even be in this gym. But damn if she didn't prove me wrong."

I watched her move, darting forward and sweeping Franco's legs out from under him. It was a thing of beauty. But as he leapt back up, and they circled one another, I couldn't help but notice that she was holding back.

"Can't even have her truly sparring with any of our women. It's too unfair. Hell, I wouldn't even put her in the ring with half our men. She'd level them."

I mulled over Clyde's words as I moved closer to the ring as if the woman had cast some sort of spell over me.

Wren stiffened, something grabbing her attention just long enough for her gloves to drop. Franco hit her in the jaw—way too fucking hard for a sparring practice.

As the woman hit the mat, Franco cursed, already crouching down. "Shit, Wren. I'm sorry. Just got caught up in the moment."

My strides ate up the distance in no time, and as I reached the edge of the practice ring, I leveled a glare at Franco. I knew my eyes had to be flashing, the silver that warned others I was a predator.

Franco stumbled back a few steps. "I didn't mean to get her so hard. I thought she was gonna block me."

Wren struggled to sit up, blinking away what I was sure was some blurriness in her vision. "I'm fine. I'm an idiot, but I'm fine."

Seeing her like this made her name seem to fit. Wren. Delicate, just like the bird.

"Come on," I said, my voice going gruff. "Let's get some ice on that."

"I'm okay," she argued instantly. "Really."

My wolf bristled. He was already on edge, wanting to rake his claws down the chest of the man who'd hurt his Little Warrior.

His?

Fuck. Was this a mating call? I'd felt them a time or two, the pull of attraction that meant someone could possibly be your mate. It wasn't a guarantee, only a sign that you were compatible.

The only certainty came from a true mating bond—the kind that showed itself the second you had skin-to-skin contact. It was said the bond sang through every nerve ending, and images of your future would flash.

I reached for Wren's elbow as she slid under the rope, trying to steady her. She stiffened instantly. I braced, waiting to feel the certainty, to see those images. But there was nothing.

My wolf growled at the lack of it all. He wanted her to be his. And I sure as hell understood the disappointment.

I shook it off, trying to pull myself together. "Come on. Let's get you to my office."

"I'm good. Really—"

"Girlie, you don't gotta listen to him, but you do gotta listen to me if you wanna keep fighting around here. His office so we can take a peek at you."

Wren's head lifted, revealing the full side of her face for the first time. I knew wounds. My brothers and I had received more than a few, so I knew how to recognize what had inflicted them. And this scar hadn't been caused by shattered glass or some freak accident. It was from a blade.

My wolf went rabid.

CHAPTER FOUR

Wren

I felt the shift before I saw it. The claws that raked my emotional shields were fiery. Anger? No, *rage*.

It battered my invisible walls, making my head throb more. How could I have been so stupid? I knew better than anyone that letting your guard down for even a second could get you killed.

Or, in this case, put you in the clutches of an overbearing wolf shifter who smelled like…fresh mint and pine. And, God, I wanted to roll around in it.

Danger.

The thought emblazoned itself in neon red in my mind. This was touch-hunger and nothing else. I was so starved for contact with my species that I must've been in some sort of lust-induced haze.

That was also my justification for allowing him to lead me down the back hall to a door I'd never seen open in my month in Crescent Creek. The man released his hold on my elbow, and I suddenly felt cold, like I'd walked into a snowstorm wearing nothing but a tank top and shorts.

He pressed his palm to some sort of reader beside the door. I'd thought the thing was a tablet that controlled the heat and air conditioning, but it was clearly some sort of high-tech lock. The knowledge had my skin bristling.

I expected my wolf to lunge to the surface, dying to break free and *run*. Instead, I found she was…purring? Wolves didn't *purr*. But that was the only way I could describe the sound emanating from her.

The man opened the door and ushered Clyde and me inside. The second I stepped across the threshold, I regretted coming with them so pliantly. Because that fresh mint and pine scent? It was all around me now, choking every breath I took.

Fucking hell.

It was almost more than I could bear. I struggled to breathe evenly and not bolt like a scared doe.

"Come on, girlie. Sit down. You look like you're about to pass out," Clyde said, pushing me toward the leather couch against the wall.

I stumbled back onto it. "I'm fine. Swear. Everyone takes a hard hit now and then."

The man frowned down at me. "You need to go to the hospital to get checked for a concussion."

If I had a concussion, it would heal in a matter of hours, thanks to my shifter half, but he didn't need to know that. "It's not a concussion. Trust me, I know what those feel like."

The other man's light-blue eyes flashed silver. "What. Does. That. Mean?"

Clyde slapped him on the back. "Easy, King. She's been fighting a long time. She's taken a knock or two."

That had the silver shifting back to pure blue. Still, there was an assessing quality there, like he was trying to put the pieces together.

"Come on," Clyde pressed. "Get her some ice and Tylenol."

The man let out a low growl. "Who's the boss around here?"

Clyde chuckled. "Don't worry. You still call the shots, but you're also freaking Wren the fuck out right now. So, go get the goddamn ice."

The man let out a chuffed breath but headed for the door.

I watched as he went, unable to look away. And for the first time, I really took him in. He wore a gray tee that loosely hugged planes of muscle and ghosted over broad shoulders. His dark jeans housed muscular thighs and were paired with scarred motorcycle boots.

He was tall—so tall I had to look up, up, up to get to his face. And that face. It was devastatingly beautiful. Thick scruff covering an angular jaw. A nose with a hint of a bump that told me it had been broken before. Dark-brown hair. And eyes I wanted to drown in. They were the sort of light blue that could hold you captive.

I stared at him for so long, the man disappeared, and I was still locked on the spot where he'd been. Right until a throat cleared. My head jerked in Clyde's direction, and I let out a curse as everything spun.

Clyde chuckled. "Never known you to be distracted by a pretty face."

"I'm not," I argued. And it wasn't a complete lie. "He's just—"

"King's a lot. I get it."

"King," I echoed, rolling the sound of his name on my tongue.

"Kingston. The owner of the gym. Been out of town working a job."

I stiffened. "He *owns* the gym?"

Clyde nodded swiftly. "The gym and a security company. They work high-level stuff. So, he travels quite a bit. I man the shop when he's gone."

A wolf shifter with a security company who owned the gym I went to daily? This was bad. So freaking bad.

And I knew I should run.

CHAPTER FIVE

Wren

Before I could get out another word, a lock clicked, and the door to the office opened again. There was something about that lock. Specifically, the fact that it seemed to automatically engage anytime someone closed the door. That meant either something valuable was in the office or Kingston was hiding something.

I tried to scan the space to see if anything stood out—a clue, a hint of what the shifter who smelled like heaven was hiding away—but my gaze got caught on the man himself: the tee pulled taut across his broad chest, and those light blues that seared me to the spot.

Kingston crossed to me in three long strides, extending a hand with an ice pack. "Here."

The single word was deep and raspy. The kind of tone that skated across my skin in a pleasant shiver and made all the tiny hairs stand up at attention.

As he leaned in to give me the ice pack, his scent intensified. *Holy hell.* The fingers of one hand dug into the couch while I took the ice with the other. "Thank you."

My voice had grit to it now. Had it really been so long since I'd felt true attraction? Or maybe it was just touch-hunger at being this close to a male who was also a wolf. I was going with option two. It was the version that made me less of a lusty loony tune.

"Put it on your jaw," Kingston ordered.

I'd been so caught up in my spiraling thoughts I hadn't bothered to apply the ice. But his demanding tone had me lifting a brow. "Bossy, much?"

Those light-blue eyes sparked silver again. But it was Clyde who spoke amid a chuckle. "You have no idea, girlie."

Kingston's lips twitched—a hint of a smile that nearly did me in. It lightened everything about the man. His focus turned to me. "Please?"

That single word sent a shiver through me, and not because I was holding an ice pack. I pressed it to my jaw.

"Thank you." Kingston set down a water bottle and two pills. "Tylenol. For the pain."

"I'm good," I said quickly. I wasn't about to take unknown pills or a drink from a stranger.

His eyes narrowed. "Why the hell not?"

I met his stare head-on. "Taking unknown substances from someone I don't know seems like a surefire way to end up chained in some creep's basement."

Something passed over Kingston's eyes, a shadow so dark it was deeper than night, pure black. A second later, it was gone. "Might've let distraction drop your guard, but at least you're street-smart."

My back teeth ground together, making fresh pain flare in my jaw. "It was a momentary lapse. It won't happen again."

"Good to hear."

Annoyance and frustration flickered low in my belly. It wasn't as if I could tell him that realizing a wolf shifter was in the vicinity had distracted me. I pushed to my feet, relieved to not feel any dizziness. "Thanks for the ice."

Kingston shifted instantly, not blocking my path exactly, but... almost. "Where are you going?"

"Home. Like I do every night."

"Let me give you a ride. You shouldn't be driving after taking a hit like that."

"Then it's a good thing I walked," I shot back.

His light-blue eyes narrowed. "You walk here at night?" he ground out.

"I can handle myself." I might've let myself get decked today, but that was beyond rare.

"I'm walking you home." Kingston spoke the words as if they were final.

I opened my mouth to argue, but Clyde cut me off. "Do me a favor, girlie, let the stubborn bastard walk you home. If you don't, I'm gonna hear about it the rest of the night, and I don't think these old bones can take it."

I pinned Clyde with a stare, but everything else in me softened. "Don't think I don't know what you're up to, gramps."

He guffawed. "You're really sockin' it to me if you're going for *gramps*."

"Only fitting when you go for *girlie*." I bent and kissed his cheek. "Thanks for always looking out for me."

Clyde's kind protectiveness meant more than he'd ever know. It was a rare and beautiful gift I'd never take for granted.

"He gets a kiss on the cheek, and I get a glare?" Kingston asked, his tone hinting at amusement.

"He's looking out for me. You're just an interfering Nosy Nelly," I said, heading for the door.

Kingston hurried to open it before I could get there. "You know how to cut someone to the quick."

I shrugged. "Just calling it like I see it."

I headed down the hallway and into the fray of the gym. The second I reached the floor, Franco was there. "You okay, Wren? I'm so fucking sorry. I just got jacked on adrenaline after you took me down and—"

I waved him off and kept moving toward my bag. "Don't worry. It happens. I shouldn't have dropped my guard."

"*He* shouldn't have been sparring at full strength," Kingston growled.

Franco winced. "You're right. Sorry, King."

Kingston jerked his head in a nod as he clapped Franco on the shoulder. "Learn from it."

I watched the interaction with curiosity. It was clear that Kingston was a dominant wolf. I could easily feel it in the air around him. And Franco was human. Kingston could've forced his submission in a dozen different ways but didn't.

That had a grudging respect sliding through me as I grabbed my bag.

"Here," Kingston said, taking it from me. "I'll carry that."

I quickly snatched it back. "No. You won't." No one took my things, even if it was some misguided attempt at chivalry.

Kingston's brows lifted, but his gaze was astute, trying to read between the lines of my words. "All right." He gave Franco a chin lift. "See you tomorrow. We gotta work on that right hook before your match."

Franco grimaced. "I know. I'm not gettin' the right angle."

"Dropping your shoulder too much. We'll tighten it up."

I was already heading for the door, not waiting for the bro fest to continue. The truth was, the more I saw Kingston's kindness toward those in his orbit, the more I softened to him. And that was the last thing I needed.

Stepping out into the crystal-clear night, I sucked in a deep breath. As the air filled my lungs, I prayed it would clear away Kingston's scent of fresh mint and pine. But particles of it still clung to me somehow.

"Ready?"

Hell. That deep, raspy tone was almost as bad as his scent.

I didn't answer; I simply started walking. I'd never been more thankful that my apartment was only two blocks from the gym.

Kingston fell into step beside me, letting the quiet of the night swirl around us. But that only lasted for so long. "You liking Crescent Creek so far?"

My gaze flicked up to him for a brief moment. Every part of me tried to take in as much of that beautiful form as possible before I forced my attention away. "Might as well ask about the weather."

Kingston chuckled, and the sound held a rasp, a grittiness that made chill bumps rise on my skin and my nipples pebble. "It is an especially lovely evening."

He wasn't wrong there. Late April in the mountains of Colorado meant the temperatures could still drop into the teens. But tonight, it was in the balmy forties. Even if it wasn't, my internal shifter heater would've fought off the cold.

As we reached the back of Arcane, I moved to pull my keys from my bag.

"Why are you going into the bar?" Kingston asked, confusion lacing his tone.

"Because I live above it."

His brows almost hit his hairline. "Seriously?"

Annoyance prickled my skin. "Yes. Do you have a problem with that, too?"

A muscle fluttered along Kingston's jaw. "No. I just—you should make sure patrons don't know that. It's not safe."

I couldn't help seeking out those light-blue eyes as I turned the doorknob. "Trust me, I've been taking care of myself for a long time."

That had a different sort of awareness settling into Kingston's features. "All right."

"Which means you don't have to follow me inside. I'm not getting kidnapped between here and my door."

I expected a lip twitch or another of those chuckles, but Kingston didn't give me either. "Just give me this, Little Warrior. Let me walk you to your door."

Given we didn't know each other, the nickname should've made me bristle and my wolf bare her teeth. But neither came. I had a feeling arguing would only force me to be in this man's presence for longer. And that was a dangerous proposition.

So, I slipped inside, letting Kingston follow. Dina always left a few lights on to illuminate my path. The soft glow was a sort of *welcome home*—the only kind I would get without any family or a mate, not even a pet to give me a purr or bark. So, I'd hold on to those particles of light the best I could.

Heading for the back stairs, the only sound was Kingston's boots hitting the floorboards. Even *that* managed to be hot somehow. I needed to get laid and STAT.

I didn't look back as I reached my door, simply slid the key into the deadbolt and twisted. I quickly darted inside, turning and blocking the entry so Kingston wouldn't see it as an invitation to enter, as well. "As you can see, I'm home safe and sound."

Kingston's gaze roamed my face, lingering on each feature as if memorizing them. "Good." He reached into his back pocket and pulled out a wallet. He slid out a business card that looked expensive—thick card stock, embossed lettering—and held it out to me. "Call me if you need *anything*."

I stared at the card like it was a snake. And maybe it was. Still, I took it. Staring down at the letters, I read: *Crescent Kingdom Security, C.E.O.*

My gaze lifted to his. "Thanks." I knew that was the best route to getting him gone. If I protested, he'd only linger.

"You're not going to use it, are you?"

I shrugged. "I guess we'll just have to see."

One corner of his mouth pulled up. "I guess so."

"Good night, Kingston."

"Good night, Little Warrior."

I closed the door, locking the deadbolt and knob before sliding the security chain into place. Then, I waited. I didn't hear any sounds of movement at first. Then there was one footstep, then another. The pace picked up, the sound heading down the stairs.

Disappointment flared in my chest, an emotion I didn't want to look at too closely. I turned around and pressed my overheated back to the door, slowly sliding to the floor. A deep loneliness settled in. The kind I rarely let take hold. But I couldn't do anything to fight it off.

Because I was alone.

And, thanks to my father, I always would be.

CHAPTER SIX

Kingston

I STARED AT THE DOOR FOR FAR TOO LONG. THAT FLIMSY PIECE of wood wouldn't do a damn thing to keep me out. But Wren's need for safety and security and her need to put space between us would.

My wolf snarled at the thought. He didn't understand those human needs. He wanted to take her back to our territory and make sure she was safely ensconced within our borders. But he also wanted to claim her.

That was new.

My wolf had wanted women before. His hunting needs were strong when they hit. But he'd never wanted anyone with any sort of permanence. And a claiming was pretty damn permanent. The kind of forever that spanned lifetimes.

My human half wasn't much better. I'd wanted to lean in and sniff Wren, press my nose to the nape of her neck, pull the scent of wildflowers and rain into my lungs, and never let go.

The need to mark her was so strong, my canines pressed against my gums at the mental image. I knew I had to walk away. If I didn't, I'd either be knocking down her door or sleeping on the floor outside. Neither was something I wanted to explain.

Humans couldn't understand shifter urges, which were sometimes motivated by senses beyond the everyday. And our protective streaks were strong and vast.

I forced myself to step away from her door. The distance was almost physically painful—the kind of agony I'd expect from a true mating bond. Only we hadn't shared that connection. Nothing more than attraction had zinged through my veins when I touched Wren. And I hadn't seen any glimpses of our future.

I shook my head. Maybe it had simply been too long since I'd taken a woman to bed. I thought about reaching out to a she-wolf friend a few towns over, but the idea had my wolf snarling. He wanted Wren and Wren only, and my human half agreed.

Hell.

Pausing at the top of the stairs, I tapped out a text. I could've reached out to the recipient of the message through the mental bonds of our pack link, but we tried not to use that unless absolutely necessary.

Me: *Need you to look into someone. Only have her first name. Wren. But she lives above Arcane and works out at Crescent Kingdom.*

A flicker of guilt niggled in my gut, but I shoved it down. Locke would never share the information he found. But I needed to know who Wren was. Had to know if she was in danger.

Just the thought had my wolf snarling, demanding we go back to her apartment. I battled him for dominance, but he eased when my phone dinged.

Locke: *On it.*

Of course, he was. And if there was any sort of electronic trail, Locke would find it.

I jogged down the stairs but pulled up short at sounds coming from the office around the corner. Quietly, I prowled behind the bar and down the hallway before a familiar scent greeted me. My muscles relaxed, and I pushed the door to the office fully open.

Puck looked up from a desk piled high with pure chaos. "What are you doing here?"

"Could ask you the same question." I arched a brow. "Trying to dig out after an explosion?"

"Oh, piss off. We're not on mission anymore." Puck's light British accent laced his words as he shoved a hand through his blond locks, the tattoos lining his forearms glinting in the light.

I chuckled. "I just don't know how the hell you find anything in…*this*."

Puck pawed through a stack of papers. "I've got my own organization system in place."

"I bet." I was honestly surprised that he was back at the bar so quickly. Arcane was his pride and joy, but Puck didn't exactly take things seriously, and we'd only just gotten back from Siberia tonight.

Puck looked up from the chaos, studying me for a moment. "You never answered me. What are you doing here? Checking up on me?"

"No." Puck might be a wild card, but he could usually be trusted around town. "Woman at the gym took a hard hit. Wanted to make sure she got home okay."

Puck's gaze narrowed on me. "Pretty sure her bed isn't atop my bar."

"That's where you're wrong."

His green eyes flared in surprise.

"Apparently, she rents the apartment above you."

"Oh, hell. I remember Dina sending me a text about that. Forgot all about it. Raven or Sparrow? Some bird name."

"Wren," I corrected. Just saying her name aloud had my gut tightening and my canines fighting to lengthen.

Puck didn't miss the struggle. A grin stretched across his face. "You like her."

I stiffened. "She's nice."

Amusement lacing his features, he sank back into the leather office chair behind his desk. "Nice, huh?"

"I think she might be in trouble."

That had the amusement on Puck's face sliding away. "What makes you think that?"

"Scar on her face that must have been inflicted by a blade. She's jumpy. Too careful."

Puck's jaw worked back and forth as he mulled that over. "Supe or human?"

My back teeth gnashed. "She's human, but her scent... It's different somehow. She smells like wildflowers and rain, yet it's wrong."

His brow furrowed as he tried to put those pieces together. "Want me to pull her lease agreement?"

I scanned his surrounding office. "Think you could actually find it in here?"

Puck flipped me off. "Do you want me to pull it or not?"

Indecision warred inside me, but what was a peek at Wren's lease when I was already having Locke look into her? "Yes." The word was out before I could stop it.

Puck sent a far-too-pleased grin my way. "You *really* like her."

"Puck," I growled.

He rubbed his hands together like some sort of Disney villain. "This is going to be so much fun."

CHAPTER SEVEN

Wren

I TUCKED MY ARCANE TEE INTO MY JEANS, SMOOTHING OUT the invisible wrinkles like I'd smoothed my hair half a dozen times. There was no denying I was on edge. Sleep hadn't come easily or for long. And when it did, it was punctuated by nightmares of Bastian finding me and dreams of Kingston that were far from nightmarish. Hours later, my skin still felt overheated.

Crouching down, I ran my fingers along the floorboards until I found the one I'd strategically loosened. Pressing on one side, I flipped it up and pulled out the worn shoebox, taking a deep breath before opening it. Inside were all the things that made me feel safe.

A pay-as-you-go phone. An untraceable tablet. Cash. Extra IDs.

I counted the dollars. It wasn't enough to get me that far, and as much as a part of me wanted to run fast and far, I knew it wasn't the smart play. There'd be wolf shifters everywhere I went. And maybe if I had one in my daily life, I wouldn't be as at risk for my beast to tip over into feral territory.

I'd heard the warnings countless times. About how going *lone wolf* could lead to insanity or your animal taking the reins permanently. I'd felt how hard I had to battle my wolf into submission each time I shifted lately. Maybe this would help her.

She let out a haughty huff in answer as if to say, *"Like that'd do the trick."*

I knew what she wanted. What a part of me wanted, too. To know what it was like to lose myself to Kingston. To feel his fingers digging into my hips as he took me. To truly let go.

But it was more than that. I craved the feeling of strong arms around me in a simple hug. To know I was safe. Cared for.

Those were the more dangerous dreams. Because they meant *trusting* someone, and that was a luxury I couldn't afford.

My eyes burned as I put everything back into place and tested the board to make sure it was secure. I'd run a check on Bastian's pack last night in an attempt to set myself at ease. There were no signs that he or anyone else was anywhere near the-middle-of-nowhere Colorado. It should've been a relief. But it hadn't eased a damn thing.

Pushing to my feet, I smoothed my shirt again and headed for the door. I took nothing with me except my phone and keys when I worked a shift. Having both allowed me to bolt to my vehicle, where I had a separate stash of IDs and cash. I always divided things. Never put everything in one spot. It was too risky.

Slipping out of my apartment, I took the time to lock both the deadbolt and the doorknob. Then, I steeled myself and headed downstairs. I wasn't sure why I felt the need to put my armor into place. We didn't open for another thirty minutes, and it wasn't like Kingston would be waiting for me.

Just thinking his name had images of one of the dreams flashing in my mind—one hand fisting in my hair, the fingers of the other digging into my flesh. His—I let out an *oomph* as I crashed into what felt like a cement wall.

Stumbling back a few steps, someone caught me by the arm to keep me from falling. The surprise of it all had my emotional shields slipping just like my damn guard had last night. The contact of the hand on my bicep had icy claws of agony ripping through me. Physical touch when my shields were down, meant that everything was intensified—the good, the bad, and the ugly. Or in this case, the tortured.

"Easy, Birdie," a deep voice said, one that was all smoke and whiskey coated in a British tenor.

I jerked my arm free, slamming up my mental shields and trying to take in the man in front of me. Nothing about his appearance or expression read *emotional agony*, but I'd felt it, nonetheless. The man opposite me was almost as tall as Kingston, and *he* had to be six foot five. This guy was broader and slightly stockier, but he was also in shape. His biceps looked like they could crack walnuts or human necks.

His blond hair was slightly disheveled as if he'd repeatedly run his fingers through it. There was thick scruff along his jaw that said he hadn't shaved in days, and those green eyes… They pinned me to the spot with a mix of mirth and concern. But it was the scent that had me frozen.

Smoky whiskey and wolf.

I stumbled back a few more steps, my fingers itching to reach for the blade hidden in the waistband of my jeans. "Who are you? We aren't open."

The man grinned, straight white teeth practically blinding me as amusement filled his expression. "I'm Puck. You must be Wren. Dina told me all about you. Well, minus that you're fucking gorgeous. But I'm not surprised there. She always leaves out the important details."

My head spun. Between his pain still ricocheting through me and the allure of his scent, I was about to lose it.

"You look like you need something to eat. Come on." Puck reached out as if to take my arm again, but I jerked away.

"Don't touch me," I snarled.

Puck instantly retreated, holding up both hands in surrender. "All right, Birdie. I've got a friend who's the same way. Hands off, I promise. But I do make a mean grilled cheese, and I feel like you could use one."

My eyes narrowed in his direction. "Who. Are. You?"

He didn't seem offended in the slightest, simply flashed that easy grin again. "I told you. I'm Puck." He tapped the Arcane emblem on his tee, which seemed far more worn than mine. "Resident bartender."

Surprise flared as my brows rose, not doing a damn thing for the headache I was currently rocking. "The one who was off climbing Mt. Kilimanjaro?"

"That was last time, but it's good that Dina's been bragging about me. She said she wouldn't miss me, but I knew she was lying."

It was clear that Puck was a charmer, someone used to talking women into anything, but his chatter was too much on top of everything else. "Could you stop talking for just a minute?"

"You're the one who keeps asking me questions, Birdie."

I snapped my mouth closed at that.

Puck inclined his head toward the kitchen and headed in that direction. Like an idiot, I followed. But if he made a move, I had my blade and my fists.

He gestured to one of the stools on the opposite side of the island. "Headache?"

Another wave of surprise hit me as I slid onto the stool. "I get migraines."

Puck winced. "I'll get you fixed right up. Caffeine, food, and pain pills."

"Over-the-counter only, and I get them from the bottle."

His green gaze roamed over me, trying to read beneath my words. The study was so similar to Kingston's that I knew they had to be from the same pack. It made sense. Both had been out of town at the same time. I wondered if they actually had a security company. Maybe it was simply pack business.

Puck bent, opened a cabinet, and grabbed something from inside. As he straightened, he slid a bottle across to me. "Here you go."

I caught it easily and read the label. Over-the-counter. That was good. I never risked anything stronger because I couldn't afford to have my reflexes dulled. The last time that'd happened, I almost ended up dead.

CHAPTER EIGHT

Puck

I COULDN'T STOP WATCHING HER. OR SCENTING HER. *FUCK*. King had been right about her fragrance. It was human but off somehow. As if someone had dulled the incredible aroma emanating from her skin. Wildflowers. Rain. And something more.

It pulled at me. More than I wanted to admit.

Normally, that sort of tug would've had me running for the hills because of what it could mean. The potential of a mating bond. The kind of connection that could mean a lifetime in chains.

But Birdie was a puzzle. Something my mind *needed* to figure out.

As she studied the bottle of pain pills, I got to work pulling out ingredients for the best damn grilled cheese I'd ever made, along with a little something else. We kept the herb mixture in one of the cabinets here in case Locke ever needed it.

He brought his laptop to the bar to work on the regular, which meant we needed to keep it in stock. I put a teaspoonful of the green substance in a glass and then poured water over it, mixing everything together. It looked disgusting but seemed to work like a charm, at least for Locke.

I set the glass in front of Wren. "Try this, too."

Her button nose wrinkled, making those stunning-as-hell turquoise eyes stand out more. "What is that?"

"An herbal tincture to help with headaches. I have a friend who gets them from staring at a screen for too long. This helps him."

"Sounds like you've got a lot of friends," Wren muttered.

I set to work grating some sharp cheddar. "I'm a charming bastard. Of course, I do."

Wren lifted the glass and sniffed the contents before sending me a piercing look. "If you're trying to drug me, I'll cut off your nuts and feed them to you."

My lips twitched. "Violent little thing. I like it." I set aside the cheese and took the glass from her, sipping the contents. I gagged. "Tastes like the inside of a gym locker, but it's drug-free."

Wren fought against a smile but finally gave in and took the glass back, downing it. She waited, clearly on edge. She eased when a couple of minutes passed and she realized she didn't feel hazy. "That was gross."

I chuckled, turning on a burner and placing a large skillet on it. I could've turned on the grill, but it seemed like a waste for just the two of us. "Don't worry, I'll cure your taste buds with the best grilled cheese known to man."

Wren arched a brow. "Don't have much of an ego at all, do you?"

I shot her my most charming grin. "Trust me, it's earned."

"I don't trust anybody."

The words seemed to slip out of Wren's mouth before she could think better of it, a little explosion of truth when her secrets were so carefully guarded.

"Easiest way not to get hurt," I agreed. I understood the urge to lock people out after a betrayal. In many ways, I still did. But I had my brothers. Not ones born of blood but those forged in the fire of battle and given freely through choice.

Our ragtag team of five was one we slowly added to over the years. But we would do anything for one another. Fight, even die. Without them, my life would be empty.

Wren studied me for a long moment. "There's only one person who will always have your back. Yourself."

I flipped both grilled cheeses over. "Not if you find the right people."

Wren shifted on her stool. I could sense something in her, something she was shoving down. A yearning, maybe.

"Sometimes, even the *right* people wear masks," she muttered.

King was right. Someone had hurt her. Broken her wings. And that sent a blaze of fury ripping through me, one that had me fighting back a shift as my wolf snarled at the thought.

The reaction nearly had me stumbling back a step. My wolf wasn't protective of women as more than a generality. He didn't want to see *anyone* face injustice or hurt. But he was wary of women, especially those we were attracted to. After everything that had happened, it made sense, but his reaction now set me on edge.

I tried to soothe the unease with the knowledge that she wasn't my true mate. There'd been no instant connection zinging through my veins when we touched. No visions of our future. This was just a healthy dose of attraction. One I'd need to deal with one way or another.

Sliding one of the grilled cheeses out of the skillet, I handed the plate to Wren. "Eat."

"They must be putting some sort of bossy juice in the water around here," she muttered.

I bit back my grin because I knew she had to be referencing her run-in with King. If anyone was over the top when it came to safety and care, it was him.

Turning the burner off on my grilled cheese, I watched Wren

take a small, tentative bite. Then she moaned. "Oh, my gods. This is amazing."

My dick stiffened to half-mast, all sorts of images filling my head of other reasons she might say those words. I was going to hell.

"Best there ever was or ever will be?" I asked hopefully.

Wren smiled. "It's up there."

"Feeling better?" I asked, noticing the lines of tension around her eyes and mouth had eased.

She set the sandwich back on the plate. "I am. Thank you."

Before I could answer, a booming voice cut me off. "Goddamn it, Puck. If you took my twenty-two, I'm going to kill—"

The door to the kitchen swung open, and everyone froze.

If there were two pack mates that Birdie wasn't ready to meet, it was the psycho twins. They weren't twins by birth but by their love of bloodshed. Not that we all didn't delve into the dark and depraved at times. But the two of them *lived* there.

Ender's assassin's gaze leveled on Wren. "Who the hell is this, and why is she hiding a blade in her belt?"

CHAPTER NINE

Wren

I FROZE THE MOMENT THE MAN WALKED INTO THE KITCHEN. It wasn't the sight of him because I was facing away from the door. It was the scent. *Wolf.* My animal perked up instantly. But, yet again, she wasn't poised to fight.

There was no sign of the feral edge I'd experienced with her lately. Instead, it was almost like a mischievous smile spread across her face. My human half didn't share her reaction. It didn't matter that the alluring combination of cinnamon and cloves joined the scent of wolf.

My fingers twitched on the table, then slid down to my side. But before I could find the hilt of my blade, fingers curled around my wrist, clamping tightly.

Oh, hell no.

I moved in one swift motion, breaking the contact by bringing my free hand down hard. I instantly slid off the stool, taking up a fighting stance.

"Ender, don't. She's a friend," Puck warned.

The man opposite me narrowed his eyes. "The hell she is."

I was used to taking stock of opponents and gauging possible threats. I could assess someone in a split second, but something about this male stalled me. Likely the fact that he was nearly six and a half feet of pure muscle. Inky designs peeked out from under the navy tee clinging to his broad chest.

He had hair I was envious of—a deep brown with caramel undertones. The majority of his head was shaved, but it was longer on the top, pulled into a haphazard man bun. His amber eyes held the same glow as his hair.

But I didn't miss how his hands were falsely relaxed at his sides. That was a lie. The thick, long fingers were ready to do maximum damage.

"Let me pass," I ground out.

His amber eyes flashed gold. "Who are you, and which of my brothers are you after?"

For a moment, I thought he meant which of their pack I was trying to sleep with, but as one hand shifted behind his back, I knew that wasn't the case. And I wasn't about to let him reach for whatever weapon he had there.

Using my small stature and speed to my advantage, I charged forward and grabbed his arm, twisting it behind his back. "Reaching for something?"

"Uh, Birdie?" Puck began, concern bleeding into his voice. "I wouldn't do that if I were—"

His words were cut off in a flash as Ender twisted out of my hold as if it were nothing. *Dammit.* He struck out with a testing blow, which I dodged easily.

"You gave her a fucking nickname already?" Ender accused.

"I like her," Puck defended. "Which means I'd rather you not murder her in my kitchen."

I used the moment of distraction to level an uppercut to Ender's jaw. His head snapped back, but he didn't seem the least bit affected by the contact. He simply swept his foot out in an attempt to kick my feet out from under me.

I knew the move well. I'd learned it from a cantankerous trainer in New York City. I'd stayed there for six months before the crowded streets nearly did me in. My wolf and I liked fresh air and open spaces too much.

Ender landed a hook shot against my ribs, nearly stealing my breath. Yet something told me he was still holding back. I answered with a palm strike aimed at his nose, but Ender was too quick.

He moved with surprising grace for someone his size, managing to evade the worst of my attacks while dodging kitchen items in his path. We danced around the small space, back and forth, until Ender caught the edge of the skillet, sending it clattering to the floor.

"Aw, man. Seriously?" Puck moaned.

My gaze flicked to him for just a moment, but it was too long. Ender surged forward, grabbed my wrist, and pulled it behind my back in a move similar to the first one I'd used on him. Only there was no way I was escaping this grip.

"Who. Are. You?" he demanded.

I glared up at him. "I work here."

Surprise flared in Ender's amber eyes. "No, you don't."

"Dude," Puck said, sending him an exasperated look. "We've been gone for over a month. Dina hired a couple of new people."

Ender's grip on me loosened a fraction, but his eyes narrowed. "You do a background check on her?"

Panic whipped through me. I'd gotten pretty good at the fake IDs, but I didn't have a clue how to leave false trails on the internet. It was on my list of things to learn. I just hadn't gotten there yet. Hell, I hadn't even been able to finish college. No matter how many times I tried, I always seemed to get derailed.

"Jesus, End. Get a grip. And let the poor girl go," Puck ordered.

Ender released me, and I flexed my wrist, testing for pain. There wasn't any. Not really. The man's gaze swept over me, assessing but without the heat of attraction. Disappointment flared—an emotion I didn't want to look at too closely.

"Where'd you learn to fight like that?" he asked.

I lifted my chin. "If you think you've earned even one damn answer from me, you're dumber than you look."

Ender's eyes flared as Puck chuckled.

"You tell him, Birdie."

I rolled my eyes at the charmer. "I'm going to set up for the day." I grabbed the remainder of the grilled cheese still on my plate and headed for the door. "Thanks for the snack."

But even as I set to work, my mind was on the man who could fight better than anyone I'd ever seen and smelled like walking temptation. None of that was good.

CHAPTER TEN

Ender

W*HAT THE HELL WAS THAT?*

I'd come up against my share of female fighters. In my line of work, it wasn't uncommon to have a woman try to take out a target. Especially a beautiful one. Someone who could go unsuspected because the entire room was too focused on her face or body. They didn't notice when she slipped poison into a drink or a blade between someone's ribs.

My back teeth ground together. *A blade.* Like the one the girl had hidden at her waist.

"What the fuck is wrong with you?" Puck accused.

I turned to look at my pack mate, but it took more effort than I wanted to admit. My gaze was still focused on the door the woman had slipped out of. "Me? You're the one leaving yourself open to attack."

Puck stared at me for one beat, then two. Finally, he let out a sigh and bent to pick up the skillet and grilled cheese that were now scattered on the floor. "As you can see, I'm perfectly fine, and my virtue is intact."

I scoffed. "Pretty sure you lost your virtue along with your virginity when you were all of fourteen."

"Thirteen, actually," Puck said, sniffing the sandwich.

"Don't even think about eating that, you heathen."

Puck glared at me. "Doesn't smell like anything's on it."

"You're an animal."

He just shrugged, tossed the grilled cheese into the trash, and started the process of making another.

I watched him move around the kitchen, grating more of that ridiculously expensive sharp cheddar he insisted on buying. Knowing the life of privilege Puck had grown up in, it was surprising that he was the chef of the group. But he loved it, and the rest of us never complained.

"Tell me about her." It wasn't a question, and Puck arched a brow at the demand in my tone.

"You know, you could always ask nicely. You need to work on your playing-with-others skills."

"Jesus," I muttered. "Pretty please, will you tell me about this woman who *conveniently* got a job at *your* bar, who carries a knife in her belt, and could be an assassin sent by any one of our enemies?"

Puck sprinkled the cheese onto the two thick slices of bread, not answering me.

"Puck," I barked. "Have you forgotten about the dark mage clan we just dismantled, the human MC we took down before that, or the fucking Red River pack?"

His gaze flicked up to me. I saw the concern there and knew I'd made a misstep. Puck hid his empathy under layers of charm and humor, but he cared deeply for each and every one of us. He and King were the worriers of the group, and I'd let something slip that I shouldn't have.

"Is there any word on Red River?" he asked, his voice dropping.

I was usually good at hiding my reactions and stilling my emotions. You had to be when you were taking out a target from a hundred yards or pretending you were completely unassuming so you could take them out up close. But now, just the name of that vile pack had claws lengthening from my fingertips and fur rippling across my forearms.

"Locke's back on it now that we're home." My voice sounded relatively normal, but Puck didn't miss the strain.

"You know I'll help however I can," he assured me.

"I know," I clipped. "But right now, you can help by telling me what that girl's deal is."

There was something about the woman's scent. It was human but not quite…right. The urge to lean in and fucking *sniff* her when I had her pinned had almost been too much to bear. Even now, the scent of wildflowers and fresh rain still clung to me as if particles of her had embedded themselves in my skin.

Puck sighed and then pointed the spatula at the stool the girl had vacated. "Sit. I don't trust you not to fuck up this grilled cheese with your rage responses."

I let out a snort but went along with the request. As I took a seat on the stool, the scent of wildflowers and rain grew stronger because she'd been seated here for a while. *Dammit.* If I moved now, it would give away that the scent affected me, and I wasn't about to give Puck that nugget of intel. So, I simply shoved her empty plate to the side.

"Her name is Wren, and she started here about a month ago. Dina said she came in inquiring about the help-wanted sign and ended up renting the apartment above, too."

My head tipped back, and I stared at the ceiling as if I had X-ray vision and could see through the plaster and framing to the space above. What would it say about her? Pink and girlie? I didn't think so. Black and edgy? It wasn't that either.

The name *Wren* fit her. There was an earthy air to her that seemed to ground. But there was also a wild defiance to her.

She hadn't shown a single ounce of fear when faced with me. And just about everyone usually did.

"King's having Locke look into her," Puck went on.

"King met her, too?" That had the hairs on the back of my neck bristling. We'd been back for less than twenty-four hours. How was this woman so entrenched in our pack already?

"She trains at his gym. I guess she took a hard hit last night, and he wanted to make sure she got home okay."

I'd just bet she had. That was a classic con move—playing the injured female so she could get in close and do some serious damage.

Puck flipped one grilled cheese onto a fresh plate and slid it to me. "Chill. She's not a threat." He frowned. "Though she did threaten to slice my balls off and feed them to me. Maybe I should've taken that more seriously since she had a knife."

"You think?" I gritted out, then took a bite of the grilled cheese. It was the perfect mixture of cheddar with a bite, fresh bread, and seared butter.

Puck pushed his own sandwich onto the cutting board and sliced it in two before taking a bite. "I wouldn't make a move there. King seems protective."

"When isn't King protective?" He was forever swooping in to save the wounded birds. As if that would miraculously bring his sister back. "I'll figure out her deal."

"End," Puck warned. "Don't kill her."

The request had me stiffening. "Since when do you care who I kill?"

Puck shrugged. "I dunno, there's something about her. I like her."

Fuck.

This was exactly why I should kill her right now. Our lives didn't come with picket fences and two-point-five kids. Anyone linked to us was a risk—for them *and* for us.

CHAPTER ELEVEN

Wren

As I rounded the corner, I caught sight of Dina moving around the bar. Although only about a third of the space was occupied, she had her hands full, collecting empties and depositing fresh drinks.

"Are you sure you're okay with me going? I can stay and help," I offered, adjusting my duffel on my shoulder.

Dina waved me off. "You worked a double yesterday. *Go.* But maybe first, see if you can get that register unstuck. I hate those tablet doohickeys."

I chuckled and moved behind the bar. "I'll do my best, but you know tech isn't always my thing either."

When the new register system was delivered a week into my working here, Dina had cursed up a blue streak. I'd managed to get it set up and working, but she still struggled now and then.

I tapped the tablet's screen, but nothing happened except a flicker of movement. I frowned. Maybe there was a bug or something. I pressed the button on the side to turn it off. Because when all else failed, reboot. Still, nothing happened.

"Crap," I muttered.

"Can, um, I help?" The hesitant voice came from the other side of the bar and down a couple of seats.

I hadn't noticed the man when I came downstairs, but I should've. He was incredibly handsome, though, in a way that said he didn't want people to notice. He was leanly muscled and wearing a dark-blue flannel. Black-framed glasses hid enchanting gray eyes.

As I focused, I scented wolf. It didn't surprise me this time. There was clearly a pack in the area. The only reason I hadn't noticed was because the space was clogged with Puck's scent. That infuriating charmer of a wolf had worked the bar all day, teasing and toying with every person in Arcane. Including me.

The man sent me a hesitant smile and something about it felt like a warm hug. Like arms being wrapped around me that I could sink into and forget all my problems.

The backs of my eyes burned. Gods, I hadn't felt that in years. Probably not, since I'd spent half a year in California and allowed myself the luxury of a single friend. But I'd disappeared out of Hayden's life, too, when the town got a few too many supernatural eyes on it.

I couldn't risk it, not when I knew Bastian was still looking for me. I shook off thoughts of all I was missing and everything I was terrified of and focused on the person offering help. "I think it's glitching. I can usually turn it off and back on, and everything's good. Seems not this time."

The man nodded. "If you unhook it from the dock, I can take a look."

I gave him a quick, assessing stare. The last thing I needed was to get Dina's tablet stolen. But the man had a laptop open in front of him on the bar along with his burger, and a messenger bag sprawled on the stool. He wouldn't leave all that for a tablet.

Disconnecting the device from the dock, I walked it down to

the man. As I got closer, more of his scent hit me. Spiced chocolate, like the drinks I used to treat myself to once a month in New York. And it held the same sort of comfort. Like wrapping my hands around a cup of Mexican hot chocolate as snow fell softly around me.

Gods, that was a ridiculous thought. I shook it off and handed the man the device. He took it, and it was almost like he was trying not to move too fast. *Interesting.*

He also didn't seem to want to make eye contact. But I kept my focus on him as he tapped the screen a couple of times, registering the glitch.

"When's the last time you updated this thing?" he asked, his voice matching the soft feel of his presence.

"We only got it about three weeks ago. So, never?"

He nodded, his brown hair swooping across his forehead. "There was a critical update about a week ago. That's why you're running into this issue."

"How the heck am I supposed to update it when it's frozen?" I asked.

His lips twitched—lips that were a reddish berry color and only accentuated his strong, stubbled jaw. "We can force a reboot. Just need to press these two buttons and hold." He demonstrated with the power and home buttons. Before long, the screen went black and then began rebooting.

"A magician," I mumbled.

He shrugged. "This is just kind of my wheelhouse."

Dina moved up behind him and bent to kiss his cheek. "My hero. Thank you, Locke."

His face flamed. "No problem, D."

Locke. An interesting name. One that fit him. I had the bizarre urge to ask him where it had come from, but I didn't ask people questions. Didn't take those risks. Because if you asked someone about their life, they generally asked about yours. And I couldn't give them answers, not honest ones anyway, and the lies still tended to give something away.

Plus, they got old. Nothing about me was true. Nothing except the name I'd held on to, which wasn't even my real name yet had become the most truthful part of me. The piece of my mother I still had.

Her face flashed in my mind. Her kind eyes were the same sea-blue as mine. I knew I'd gotten my empathy from her. It didn't matter that it was a rare shifter trait; I knew her kind spirit and caster magic had burned the gift into me. And even though it felt like a curse most of the time, I'd hold on to it with all my might because it felt like holding on to her.

"Are you okay?"

The quiet voice snapped me out of my walk down memory lane. "Sorry, just crossing things off my mental to-do list."

Locke frowned, looking frustrated as he seemed to search for the right words. "I'll get this fixed and back to D."

Something told me he hadn't wanted to say that, but I still nodded. "Thanks again."

"No problem." His gaze had already dropped.

And losing sight of those stormy gray eyes felt like a vicious blow. Regardless, I just kept on moving. Fighting through untold pain wasn't anything new.

CHAPTER TWELVE

Wren

THAT SAME FAMILIAR SYMPHONY HIT MY EARS AS I stepped inside Crescent Kingdom. I closed my eyes for the briefest moment to soak it all in. Gods, I needed this. To lose myself in working my muscles to the point of exhaustion. As a reminder that I could protect myself now. And to burn off a little of the energy brewing inside me at being in the presence of wolves again.

Wolves that pulled at different elements of attraction in me—dangerous attraction.

"Birdie," a familiar British voice called.

My eyes flew open, and I nearly swallowed my tongue. Puck stood by a heavy bag, wearing nothing but sneakers, workout shorts, and boxing gloves. His tanned skin was on complete display, intricately inked artwork covering the canvas.

My gaze caught on different elements: a compass rounding

his forearm, the word *truth* curving around it, and a scene of five wolves along his rib cage.

"You're staring," Puck singsonged. "Does that mean you like me?"

I jerked out of my lusty haze and glared at him. "Just in shock over that shitty form."

"Told you that hook was getting lazy," Kingston said as he strode across the gym toward me. He, too, wore workout shorts that hung low on his hips, but thankfully, he had on a T-shirt with the gym's logo across the chest. "What are you doing here, Wren?"

I blinked at him a few times. "Uh, not trying to check out a library book."

Puck chuckled and strode over to us. "She's got you there, boss."

Kingston's pale-blue eyes hardened like glittering diamonds. "You took a hit to the head. You should be taking at least a week off."

I fought the urge to roll my eyes. "I'm fine. Trust me."

I'd been back to one hundred percent hours later, but that wasn't something I could tell Kingston. Instead, I lied. "He didn't get me as hard as you thought."

Kingston let out a low growl. It was so quiet that human ears wouldn't have been able to pick up, but I did. And so did my wolf. She practically *preened*, loving the alpha vibes clogging the air.

I had to steel myself against them because even though I'd taught myself to fight and withstand others' dominance, my animal half was a naturally submissive wolf. It came with the ability to take on others' emotional pain. You couldn't do that if you were also trying to dominate them.

Kingston let out a long breath as if trying to get himself under control. "I saw Franco hit you. It wasn't just a sparring blow. It packed heat."

"I know myself and my body. If you want to check my pupils for a concussion, go ahead, but I'm training today."

Puck looked back and forth between Kingston and me, a grin

playing on his lips. "You can kick my ass anytime, Birdie. I volunteer as tribute."

Kingston smacked the back of Puck's head. "Shut up, you overgrown toddler."

Their interaction had me fighting a smile. "While you two figure out your interpersonal dynamics, I'm going to warm up."

I crossed to the far wall, setting my bag down and grabbing my water bottle out of it. Then I headed for an empty treadmill. I eased into a slow jog, feeling my muscles loosen as I cracked my neck. Gods, it felt good to move.

It wasn't long before the treadmill next to me started up. My gaze flicked to the newcomer, who could've taken any of the other open machines, leaving space between us. Puck shot me a grin that did something to my insides.

"Decided I could use a run."

I let out a snort that was in no way ladylike. "Has anyone ever told you that you have stalker tendencies?"

Puck chuckled as he picked up to a run. "A loveable stalker, right?"

"Whatever helps you sleep at night." But I couldn't deny that I liked his presence. His scent. His whole aura. And my wolf had been more at ease in the past twenty-four hours than over the past decade. Somehow, these men made her feel like part of a pack, even though we weren't.

Just that simple thought sent a pang through me. And for the first time, I realized I wanted that. To belong. It might be far too risky for me to actually reach for it, but it didn't stop me from wanting it with every fiber of my being.

"Birdie?" There was concern in Puck's voice now.

"Oh, were you talking?" I asked, forcing humor into my voice. "I thought I heard the buzz of a gnat."

Puck chuckled. "Not only is she violent, she's vicious, too. I think I'm in love."

I scoffed, slowing the treadmill to an easy jog. "Pretty sure I saw you fall in love half a dozen times while slinging drinks today."

"Charming," Puck corrected. "I was charming them, not falling in love with them. Helps with the tips."

I slowed to a walk, stretching my arms over my head. I bet it *did* help with tips. But I'd never mastered more than polite service in that arena. Never had with strangers.

Finally, I stopped the treadmill and hopped off. I moved my body through a series of light stretches until I heard a groan behind me. My head snapped around to find Puck staring at my ass.

I scowled at him, flipping up my middle finger. "Eyes off the goods."

Puck just chuckled and jogged over. He reminded me of a puppy. A too-hot-for-his-own-good puppy, but a puppy, nonetheless.

"How about some partner stretching? I can help you really feel that burn—"

"Puck," I warned, but my head filled with all sorts of creative images. *Shit.*

He held up both hands in surrender. "Sorry, sorry."

"How about I give you some real full-body contact instead?" I asked with a smirk.

Puck's green eyes flashed gold briefly, his wolf rising to the surface. "Told you, Bridie. You can kick my ass any day of the week. Let's spar."

A low growl sounded just loud enough for my shifter hearing to pick up on it as Kingston moved into our huddle. "If she's sparring with anyone, it's going to be me."

CHAPTER THIRTEEN

Wren

IT TOOK EVERYTHING IN ME TO KEEP MY WOLF IN CHECK. SHE might be submissive, but she had a reaction to men trying to exert their authority over her. Or, in this case, just being generally bossy and overprotective.

I straightened from my stretch, doing everything I could to keep a nonchalant look on my face. "I don't know, King. Are you sure I'm not going to hurt you?"

The use of his nickname, the one I'd heard Clyde call him, was purposeful. A false sense of connection *and* a challenge.

Kingston's eyes flashed silver. "Little Warrior, you're playing with fire."

I shrugged carelessly. "Prove it." And with that, I grabbed my water bottle and gloves and headed to the ring.

"Fuck, King. I'm in love. Please, let me fight her," Puck begged.

I bit my lip to keep from laughing as the practice ring emptied. Franco and Juan climbed down, both stopping by me.

"You doing okay?" Franco asked, examining my face for any signs of bruising. There probably would've been, but my shifter healing took care of that quickly.

"I'm all good. Promise. You barely got me," I assured him.

Franco's shoulders relaxed with relief. "Happy as hell to hear that."

"Still lookin' perfect from where I'm standing," Juan added.

Another growl sounded behind me, but this one was louder, a decibel that human ears could clearly hear as both Franco and Juan took big steps back.

"Sorry, boss," Juan called. "Hands off. I got it."

I turned to face Kingston, my eyes narrowing. "What was that about?"

"He was being inappropriate."

My brow arched. "And Puck wasn't?"

"Don't worry, I'll be putting Puck in his place, too."

I scoffed and then climbed into the practice ring. "I don't need your protection, Kingston."

I could take care of myself. And that fact hadn't come easily. I'd had to break myself in so many ways. Remake myself into someone who never cowered. It had taken years. But I'd gotten there.

Kingston ducked between the ropes, moving to the opposite side of the ring. He stretched his neck from one side to the other, and I heard a faint pop. Then he reached behind his head and pulled his Crescent Kingdom tee off in one fluid motion.

My brain short-circuited. I hadn't expected the overprotective, by-the-book Kingston to be covered in ink. Intricate designs played over his shoulders and pecs, ran down his ribs, and disappeared beneath his shorts.

Holy hell.

I finally forced my gaze up to his face and locked eyes with him. Those icy blues were already on me. He'd seen me taking in every inch of the inked skin and hadn't done a thing to stop me. My wolf let out that low purr again. She wanted to do more than look.

I tore my focus away from Kingston. I needed to get it together and prove that I could handle myself. That need was born of almost a decade of being in a monster's clutches. But more than that, it was for me.

I pulled my sparring gloves on and cracked my fingers. Closing my eyes for a moment, I took the time to center myself, a reminder of everything I fought for rising. When I turned back around, I didn't see Kingston as a shifter I felt the brutal tug of attraction toward. I didn't see him as the kind man making sure I got home safely. I saw him as my opponent, nothing more and nothing less.

Kingston's gaze swept over my face, a hint of surprise showing. But he still stepped into the center of the ring, holding out his gloved fist.

I met him in the middle, feeling all eyes in the gym on us. As our knuckles connected, I met his stare dead-on. "Don't hold back."

Kingston's expression flashed with surprise again, but he didn't give me words. Instead, he turned to Clyde. "You call it."

"You got it, boss."

A second later, a whistle blew.

My weight instantly shifted to the balls of my feet. Being small had its advantages and disadvantages. One of the pros was that I was lighter on my feet and could move faster. I knew I'd need every ounce of that with Kingston.

We circled each other for a moment, both trying to register how the other moved. Kingston had surprising grace for his size, similar to Ender's in the kitchen earlier. It made sense, given they were from the same pack. They likely trained together regularly.

But that also gave me information. Kingston would probably pull some of the same moves Ender had. I filed that knowledge away in the back of my head while still trying to stay in the present.

Kingston sent out a testing jab, one painfully easy to block. I answered with a jab of my own, but it packed more heat. Kingston didn't move to block it fully and let out a soft *oomph* at the contact.

A look of appreciation filled his face, one I wanted to roll my eyes at. "Come on, King. Put a little effort into it," I challenged.

That had the man opposite me picking up his pace. But still, his hits and kicks lacked any real heat. "Kingston," I growled, putting everything I had into a blow to his ribs. "Fight back."

His jaw hardened. "I don't make a habit of hitting women."

That only fueled the fire. "Then don't look at me as a woman. Look at me as someone who's about to kick your ass."

I heard some hoots from the crowd.

"You'll be in good company, boss," Juan called. "Pretty sure she's kicked all our asses at some point."

I didn't want to lose focus, but I couldn't help the slight twitch of my lips. It was enough for Kingston to get off a blow to my ribs. I managed to dodge the worst of it, but the slight sting was a gift—the gift of respect.

"That's more like it," I said around my mouthguard.

We moved in earnest then, dodging and weaving, picking up speed. The rest of the world slipped away until it was just King and me. It was my favorite feeling: nothing but the present, no past wounds and scars, no fears about the future. There was only here and this.

My knee lifted in a blow to Kingston's ribs. He grunted and answered with a move that sent me to the mat, flat on my back. I was usually quick enough to roll to my feet and not let anyone trap me there because the mat was where my size worked against me.

But King was too fast. He was on top of me in a flash, pinning my arms above my head. I bucked my hips, trying to get into a position that would free me, but there was no use.

"Tap out," Kingston growled.

I gritted my teeth and only fought harder.

His grip on my wrists tightened. "Tap out."

I let out a sound of frustration but used my fingers to tap the side of his hand as I gave him the words. "Tap out."

Kingston was off me in a flash, pulling me to my feet. "You've got talent, Little Warrior."

The warm feeling of that praise swirled around me as I took my mouthguard out and stuck it back in its case. "Thanks for actually fighting back." Though I had a feeling what I'd seen was only the tip of the iceberg.

"Told you, boy," Clyde called from his spot at the ropes.

The crowd that had gathered around us sent up whoops and hollers, along with some good-natured shit talking. But one person pushed toward the front of that crowd, and I froze. His hair was dark, just shy of black, and hung to his shoulders, framing a face that would've been devastatingly handsome if not for the ice-cold expression. His eyes were a startling blue-green, and next to one was a knife.

"Wren," he growled.

Oh, crap on a cracker.

I knew that face. I hadn't just ended up in a wolf pack's territory. I'd ended up in *The Diablos'*—a wolf pack of feral mercenaries known for their mercilessness and creativity with body disposal. I was so screwed.

CHAPTER FOURTEEN

Brix

MY WOLF PUSHED AT MY SKIN AS I SCENTED THE AIR. HE wanted out. Wanted to scent the little human whose aroma was equal parts addicting and wrong. He couldn't put the pieces together, and neither could I.

My alpha stepped between me and the focus of my wolf's fixation, a look of concern on his face. I shouldn't have been surprised that Kingston was taking a protective stance. He had a thing for broken birds and knew I couldn't be trusted.

But Wren didn't look quite so broken anymore. She looked stronger than the last time I'd seen her. And she sure as hell had more fire.

"Do you know her?" Kingston gritted out.

If I made a habit of smiling, I would've done it then. Knowing I had a piece of information that Kingston didn't have, brought me what would've felt like joy to most people. But for me, it was a flicker just beyond the nothingness I felt most of the time.

I shifted, moving so I could take in the little human. So tiny, yet she'd fought with such ferocity. I admired the hell out of that.

"She's friends with Hayden, Cillian's...partner." I left off the word *mate*, given our mixed company. Just like I omitted the part where Hayden and Cillian were dragon shifters and had four others in their bond.

I wasn't sure if Wren had that information. I assumed she didn't. But Cillian and his horde had been surprisingly protective of the little human when I asked about her four years ago. It could've simply been because their mate cherished her friendship, but maybe it was something...more.

My wolf had wanted to hunt her back then. He'd wanted to mark her as ours yet was suspicious of her all the same. That sort of combination could be lethal to someone like me.

Kingston took a step back, turning to see both Wren and me. "How do you know Hayden?"

Wren's expression turned blank. There was no longer light in her eyes or heat in her cheeks. She was nothing more than a mask of nothingness.

My beast hated it. He charged to the surface, snarling. He wanted to break free and uncover all the secrets she was hiding, claiming them for himself.

"I went to Evergreen University for a year. We had a few classes together."

I didn't miss how Wren downplayed their bond. Why was that?

It was Puck who spoke, moving in next to me. "You a genius, Birdie? That school is next level."

Curiosity coursed through his expression as he studied her, but Wren was already moving, slipping through the ropes and grabbing her water bottle. "No genius here. Clearly, since I didn't finish."

I didn't think that was the case. I had a feeling Wren was plenty smart enough to dominate in all her classes. I thought she'd run for a whole other reason.

The other fighters who'd been watching the exchange started to disperse. They weren't interested in this sort of mundane information—or what they *thought* was mundane.

But I knew better. My little human was hiding something. And I would find out what.

Puck trailed behind her like a lost puppy. "Where are you going? I thought we could all grab some grub at the diner. We've earned it after a workout like today's."

Wren shook her head, her gaze momentarily flicking to me. "Can't. I have plans tonight."

Puck stiffened. "What sort of plans?"

She shot him a look of challenge. "I'm not sure that's any of your business."

"Birdie..." he pressed.

Wren stuck out her tongue at him. "Washing my hair."

"Burn," Juan called from his spot at the heavy bag.

Wren tossed her belongings into a duffel and hauled it over her shoulder. "See you tomorrow."

Kingston moved to intercept her. "Are you okay?"

She nodded a bit too quickly. "Of course. Why wouldn't I be?"

Kingston didn't speak for a moment, his eyes searching hers. Finally, he stepped back, letting her pass. She moved in a blur of motion, heading out the door without another word.

King's voice dropped. "She's running from something."

"No shit," Puck echoed. "But fair warning, Ender's convinced she's an assassin here to kill us all."

Of course, he was. My partner in punishment and bloodshed thought everyone was out to get us. I wasn't so sure. That didn't mean I thought everyone was a saint. I was well aware of how dark the world could get. How twisted.

Kingston groaned, pinching the bridge of his nose. "I hope like hell he's not stalking her right now."

I wouldn't have been surprised if he was. That was what Ender did before deciding what punishment fit the crime. Would their death be merciful? Or slow and painful?

As if we'd conjured him by words and thoughts alone, Ender swept in through the front door, Locke on his heels, looking nervous.

"Tell them," Ender demanded.

Locke's gaze flitted among us before returning to Ender. He swallowed hard and then glanced at the door before dropping his voice. "That girl? There's no record of her existence... *anywhere.*"

CHAPTER FIFTEEN

Wren

I PACED BACK AND FORTH IN MY TINY APARTMENT. I'D TAKEN the world's quickest shower in case I needed to run. That's what I should do: run fast and far. But thinking about that had my heart clenching.

Somehow, the people of Crescent Creek had wormed their way into my heart in only a month. Clyde, with his gruff, grandfatherly affection and expert fight training. Dina, with her no-bullshit help and way of making me feel a part of something. Even Franco and Juan at the gym. It was more *belonging* than I'd had in a long time.

I worried the inside of my cheek, trying to figure out the best path forward. As much as The Diablos had a ruthless reputation, I knew they also used it for good. They'd been the ones to rescue Hayden when she was in a bad situation all those years ago, stepping in to help when no one else could.

That was a mark in the stay column. Another was that

running would only prove I had something to hide, and with hunters like these men, that was never a good idea.

I crossed to my secret floorboard and pried it up, pulling out my shoebox. I didn't reach for the cash or the IDs—none of my typical self-soothing methods. Instead, I pulled out the tablet and powered it on.

It had been set up by a hacker I'd had to pay far too much money and had things like firewalls, false IP addresses, and other technical stuff I didn't have the first clue about. But the woman had assured me that no one could trace the activity on it. And that was exactly what I needed right now.

My fingers drummed on my thigh as I waited for the thing to boot up. It was several years old, and I knew I'd have to replace it soon, which would cut into my cash reserves.

Yet another reason to stay. The steal I was getting on this apartment and the fair wages Dina paid made for an ideal setup. As long as I could convince the five nosy wolves in Crescent Creek that I was about as interesting as watching paint dry.

The tablet finally struggled to life, and I tapped on the internet browser icon. That was slow, too, taking its sweet time to load. Finally, I was able to type in the address of my old pack's domain.

The thing about being a submissive, especially one regularly used as a punching bag, was that you got good at being quiet. Between that and the fact that people had rarely noticed me, I saw things they didn't want me to.

And I stashed those little nuggets of information away, holding them close. Things like the head enforcer's login and password to the system housing the pack's movements. My father collected wolves like trophies. His most prized possessions were those with the most unique gifts.

Yet another reason it had been so important for me to hide my empathic gift from him. If he'd known about it, he would've bled me dry in a matter of months.

But Bastian also collected wolves—for sheer numbers

alone—just to exert his dominance. But the size of his pack meant it was difficult to keep track of the members and their assignments.

He'd thought he was *so* smart devising a system like this one. He even forced his wolves to be implanted with GPS trackers so he could track their movements. But what he didn't realize was that he'd also given me what I needed to stay safe.

I clicked on the tab that read *Pack Leadership*. Of course, my father didn't have himself chipped; that was too beneath him as the alpha. But I knew he never traveled alone. With his power, he'd gotten lazy. His brutal vindictiveness had protected him, but he wasn't actually strong. So, he always took at least four of his top enforcers with him, and usually his beta, as well.

I went through each of them, systematically checking their current location and movements for the past week. It took forever, but I breathed a little easier each time I saw they were nowhere near Crescent Creek, Colorado.

Finally, I clicked on the beta. A man possibly more evil than Bastian. Marcelle and my father spurred on each other's enjoyment of cruelty and suffering. Honestly, I wasn't sure who terrified me more.

Just tapping my finger on his name had my hand trembling, memories rising of the pain he'd inflicted on me in my father's quest to make me *stronger* and more dominant. Marcelle wasn't outside New Orleans like the rest of the pack. He was in New York. The Lower East Side specifically.

That knowledge had the hairs on the back of my neck standing on end. He was in a place I'd lived six years ago. I tried my best to keep my breathing even, not to spiral into a panic. New York was the largest city in the world. There could be countless reasons Marcelle was there.

But fear still dug in its icy claws. I dropped the tablet to the floor and hugged my knees to my chest. I'd done so much to battle back the fear and equip myself in case Bastian and his men ever found me. But it wasn't enough.

Because to have a prayer of escaping my father's clutches, I'd need an army at my back. And despite my flickers of belonging in Crescent Creek, these people didn't know me. Not really.

I was still totally and completely alone.

CHAPTER SIXTEEN

Ender

"YOU'VE GOT TO BE FUCKING KIDDING ME," I SNARLED at the men stuffed into King's office at Crescent Kingdom.

Our alpha sent me a look that should've scared the hell out of me, but I was too pissed off to truly take it in. My brothers were acting like lovesick fools. Even Brix, the packmate who always had my back, wasn't having a strong enough reaction to the new information about Wren.

The moniker likely wasn't even her name. Who the hell knew what it might be? She'd probably picked it as an extra layer of manipulation. The word conjured up the image of a delicate bird when it was clear she was anything but.

Kingston held up a hand, asking for silence. "If the dragons allow her to be near their mate, they obviously trust her."

"They do," Brix agreed, though I heard uncertainty in his tone. "They were almost…protective of her."

"So, she has something on them. Something they don't want to get out," I argued. That was the only thing that made sense.

Puck scoffed. "If that was the case, Wren would be dead, not chilling in Crescent Creek."

My back teeth ground together. How could he be so blind to what was happening right in front of him? "She could have a fail-safe in place. If something happens to her, information goes public." We all knew the dragons had plenty they didn't want getting out.

"Or maybe they've lost their edge. They've been softening since meeting their mate," I spat. Because that's what happened when you let someone in to that degree. They owned you.

Puck snorted this time. "Tell that to Cáel. I'm pretty sure he'd peel the skin from your bones."

"Whatever," I muttered.

King let out a low growl, making his frustration with me clear. But he turned his focus on Locke. "Walk us through the searches you ran."

Locke shifted uncomfortably on the leather couch. He hated being the center of attention, but he flipped open his laptop and struck a few keys. The thing was like a shield protecting him from the outside world.

"I did all the usuals: DMV, IRS, court system, law enforcement databases. Nothing matches that name with her photo."

It was my turn to let out a growl. "Innocent people don't hide their identity like that."

"Says the guy with two dozen false identities in his safe," Puck muttered.

I glared at him. "I'm not exactly innocent, brother."

"But she is," he spat back.

"How can you be so sure?" I demanded. "Can you risk *everything* because of it?" We had a list of enemies a mile long, and they'd all love to insert a sleeper.

Puck shifted uncomfortably. "I don't know how to explain it. I just *know*. It's like there's a certainty in my bones or something."

King leaned back, resting on the edge of his cluttered desk. "I have the same sense. There's an urge to protect her."

I scoffed. "You have the urge to protect every female with any hint of being broken."

The room went silent for a beat, and then Kingston's low, menacing growl lit the air. It was a damn good thing the walls were made of cinder blocks. Otherwise, the gym's patrons would've thought there was a wild beast in their midst. And they would be right.

I muttered a curse under my breath. I'd crossed a line, and I knew it. We might acknowledge the fact outside of King's presence but never in front of him. Because the truth was, he'd been through worse than the rest of us in so many ways.

We'd all lost people, been betrayed, but Kingston had been tortured on top of it. By a little thing called hope being dangled in front of him. When his sister was taken, he'd done everything he could to get her back. He would've paid any price, even his life.

But none of that was good enough for Red River. All they wanted was more. Power. Money. Destruction. And by the time we found Natasha, it was too late.

I ducked my head, tilting it to bare my neck in a sign of submission and apology. But I gave him the words, too, because he deserved them. "I'm sorry, King. I crossed a line."

The alpha energy eased a fraction, making everyone in the room let out a breath.

Puck smirked. "How hard is it for you to say the s-word? Sounds like someone pulling a tooth."

Locke choked on a laugh, and I sent him a dirty look that shut him right up. "You guys truly don't think it's convenient that this woman showed up right after we left to deal with the dark mages? She inserted herself into half our pack businesses without our permission or knowledge."

"Speak for yourself," Puck interjected. "Dina kept me in the know."

It was my turn to let out a growl, but mine was one of

frustration. I guess I should've been grateful that Wren hadn't tried to get a job at Brix's and my tattoo studio. Then again, if she'd made a home at Forsaken, I would've had the pleasure of ripping it out from under her.

It had to be by design that the woman had targeted two of our seemingly softer pack members. In reality, they were anything but soft, but from the outside, someone might think they were. She likely would've tried for Locke, too, but he didn't work anywhere she could infiltrate.

I sent a glare in Puck's direction. "You had no idea what was making a home in your midst."

He rolled his eyes. "Giving a hardworking woman a job and a place to stay when she clearly needed it... How dare Dina?"

My back teeth ground together as a new wave of annoyance flared.

"Guys," Locke cut in.

All our gazes cut to him. He rarely interrupted. It only meant the attention would be focused in his direction.

He swallowed hard. "Ender's so caught up in her being a threat, but what if she's running from something? What if *she's* in danger?"

There was a shift in the air, rage filling it, coming from so many different directions I couldn't pin them all down. But it was clear that my pack hated the idea.

Even if that was the truth, it still meant Wren was a risk. Because she could bring that trouble right to our doorstep.

CHAPTER SEVENTEEN

Wren

"ORDER UP," GARY CALLED OUT THE PASS-THROUGH window.

I instantly slid off my stool, where I was rolling silverware, grateful for a more active task. It didn't matter that I'd done a ten-mile run this morning in my human form. I wasn't about to risk shifting with The Diablos in the vicinity. But even with that run, I was still twitchy and on edge, waiting for one of the wolves to show and blow my cover sky high somehow.

Grabbing the two plates of food, I headed for one of the only two occupied tables. It was still early, only half past eleven, but a few regulars preferred this time.

"Here you go, Amos," I said, sliding the patty melt in front of the man who looked to be in his mid-eighties and rocked a bow tie every time he came in.

"Thank you, darlin'." He shot me a grin that deepened the lines on his face.

"And for you, Miss Ginger." I put the cheeseburger in front of her.

She sent me her megawatt smile. "You're the best."

"That's how I like to start my day. Can I get you any refills?"

Ginger glanced at their glasses. "I think we're good. What do you think, honey bunches of oats?"

I struggled not to laugh. She called Amos a different, over-the-top nickname every time they were in here, but he just looked at her like she hung the moon. The thread of humor I felt faded, melting into longing.

They'd told me they'd been together since high school. Never even dated another soul. And you could see how in love they were. I wondered what that was like. To know without a shadow of a doubt that you'd found your person and have them know everything about you.

"All good over here, my love," Amos assured her.

"Just flag me down if you need anything else, and I'll be back to check on you in a bit," I said, shoving the longing down.

I checked on the other patrons, a mother-daughter duo, and then headed back to roll more silverware. I lost myself in the routine of it, trying to think about what I was missing or what risks lay ahead. As the bell over the door jingled, I lifted my head to welcome the new customers.

Only they weren't customers. At least, one of them wasn't.

I nearly swallowed my tongue as Puck and Locke strode in. Puck was clad in black jeans, a white tee, and a leather jacket. The James Dean look fit him a little too well. His blond hair looked slightly darker, and I realized it was because the strands were still wet.

That knowledge sent my brain into overdrive, imagining all the ways it could get into that state. And thinking about Puck in the shower was not something I needed.

Locke moved in behind him. A hint of stubble adorned his

angular jaw, and his gray eyes gleamed behind his glasses. The kindness there had longing flaring back to life.

He wore dark jeans and what looked like hiking boots, paired with a flannel over a white tee—the tee just hinting at the muscle beneath. He looked like a billionaire tech genius with a second home in some ritzy mountain town.

My wolf perked right up at their presence, preening and pacing back and forth in front of her metaphorical cage. *Great, just great.*

Puck shot me a megawatt grin. "Birdie, did you miss me?"

I blinked back at him. "Uh, it's been less than twelve hours."

Locke choked on a chuckle, trying to cover it with a cough.

"So?" Puck huffed. "That's an eternity for a love like ours."

Ginger perked right up at that. "Love, huh?"

Puck crossed to her and dropped a kiss on her cheek. "She is my one and only, Ging, but she refuses to accept my undying devotion."

Amos chuckled. "Sounds like the girl has some sense to me."

"Amos, how could you?" Puck asked with mock hurt.

Locke ignored his partner in crime and took a seat at the booth in the far corner, pulling out his laptop. I took that as my excuse to avoid Puck's joking advances and grabbed a menu, taking it over to Locke. "Here you go," I said, setting it in front of him.

He smiled but still didn't meet my gaze. "I have it memorized."

My brows lifted at that. Even if Locke was a daily visitor to Arcane, the menu was pretty vast. "Impressive."

He shrugged. "I'll take a BLT and a cherry Coke."

That had me grinning. "I'm a cherry Coke gal myself."

"Good taste," Locke muttered, barely audible.

I grabbed the menu. "I'll get your order in and be back with that cherry Coke."

As I headed toward the kitchen, the bell over the door jingled again, and three women entered. I'd seen them a handful of times while working here but had always kept my distance as much as possible. They seemed to spend all their time talking badly about everyone in their orbit. And that always made me wary.

I opened my mouth to tell them to grab a seat and I'd bring them menus, but the redhead cut me off by letting out a squeal. "Puck! You're back!" She gave him an exaggerated pout. "Why didn't you text me and tell me you were home?"

Puck winced as he took in the women, and I swore I saw a hint of fear in his eyes. "Hey, Cressida. Good to see you."

The awkward formality told me this was definitely someone Puck had fucked and regretted. A burn lit somewhere deep as my wolf let out another low growl. She didn't like this female to begin with, but she liked her even less, knowing the history Cressida shared with Puck.

Not my business.

I said the words over and over as I headed toward the pass-through window. Puck could be in charge of that table. It wasn't like he'd be slinging a whole bunch of drinks at this hour.

I pinned the page from my order pad to the wheel. "Got a BLT for you, Gary."

He let out a harrumph as he ambled over to grab it. "I hear squealing. Does that mean the daughters of Satan are here?"

It was my turn to choke on a laugh. "Gary," I chided.

He just met my gaze with a challenging stare. "Tell me it's not accurate."

I couldn't. So, I just pressed my lips together to keep from laughing and headed for the bar.

I tried to focus on the task at hand—a cherry Coke for Locke. But we didn't do just any sort of cherry Cokes here. We made them with flavored syrup and maraschino cherries.

"Birdie," Puck hissed.

My gaze flicked briefly to him as I grabbed a tall glass. "Yes?"

"Can you take these menus to table five?"

"Busy. I'm afraid you'll have to handle that."

Puck moved in closer, the heat of his body bleeding into mine. "I'm not above bribery. What'll it take?"

I grabbed the ice scoop and poured some cubes into the glass. "I'm afraid you can't afford me."

"Birdie..." he ground out.

Moving to the rows of syrups, I grabbed the cherry and poured it all over the ice. "I didn't take you for a chicken."

"I'm not," Puck said, shoulders straightening, making the planes of muscle beneath his tee even more evident. Then, he sighed. "Okay, fine. This is the one instance where I am a chicken shit, scaredy cat, piss-my-trousers night-light-needer. Now, will you take pity on me?"

A laugh bubbled out of me. It couldn't be helped. But as I turned to head for the soda gun, I stopped in my tracks because Puck was staring at me like I'd grown a second head. "What?"

He blinked a few times, seeming to come back to himself. "Don't think I've ever heard you laugh. It's fucking beautiful."

Pleasure and pain slid through me, but I shoved it all down and reached for the soda gun. I shot Coke into the glass and then grabbed three cherries for a garnish. "I'll get the bitch squad. There's no need to kiss my ass."

"I wasn't—"

But I was gone before Puck could say another word. No matter what that word might've been, I knew I couldn't handle it. I moved to the table of women first and set down three menus. "Here you go, ladies. I'll be right back to take your drink orders."

"You should take it now," the brunette huffed. I was fairly certain her name was Dara.

"We'd like to request Puck as our server. He and I are *good* friends. I'm sure you understand," Cressida cooed.

Vom. Still, I forced a smile. "I'm sorry. Puck is busy at the moment and asked me to take your table. I'm sure he'll stop by if he has time."

Cressida's green eyes narrowed on me. "How do *you* know Puck?"

"I don't," I said, turning and heading for Locke's table. It wasn't a lie. I didn't know Puck from Adam. Which made the reaction of my body, mind, and wolf to all of this nonsensical. I had no attachment to Puck.

I slid the Coke onto the table in front of Locke. "Here you go. Your food should be out soon."

Locke studied the drink. "Three cherries?"

I grinned. "I was feeling generous."

Locke's gaze slid to the trio of women. "You handle them well."

I shrugged. "Meanies don't faze me."

That was the best term for them. It didn't matter if their cruelty made its way to the surface through rude comments and backstabbing or violence and torture, the root of it was always the same. And it meant my emotional shields had to be extra strong when they were around. If the women stayed too long, I'd end up with a migraine for sure.

"You sure?" Locke pressed, his gaze flicking to my face briefly.

It was as if he could get every shred of information he needed from that sliver of a second. And then his gaze was gone again. The moment he broke contact, I missed the connection.

"They won't get the best of me," I promised.

I forced myself back to the table of women. "What can I get you to drink?"

They stared at me with a mixture of expressions but kind of looked as if they'd been sucking on lemons.

"Diet Coke," the blond named Siena said.

"Same," Dara clipped.

Cressida drummed her fingers on the table. "I'll take a Diet Sprite."

She knew we didn't carry that here. She came in for happy hour drinks with friends on the regular. Still, I forced a pleasant expression. "I'm sorry, we don't have that. The only diet drink we have is Coke."

Those fingers stopped. "Such a shame. I'll take a club soda with lime. But I want Puck to make it."

Jesus. This was a bit much. And it honestly made me feel uncomfortable. "Can't guarantee that, but I'll do my best."

Cressida let out a haughty huff. "If he doesn't make it, then I don't want it."

"Your choice," I muttered, heading for the bar and kitchen area.

Puck hovered behind the mahogany structure, prepping lemons and limes for the day. "How bad?"

"Your girlfriend wants a club soda with lime, but only if you make it."

He froze, turning slowly to me as I grabbed three tall glasses and set them on the bar. "Are you serious?"

"You really know how to pick 'em," I muttered.

"It was *one* time, and I was nearly blackout drunk. It had been a rough few weeks, and I just—I did something super fucking stupid."

Something about the *rough few weeks* tugged at my attention. I glanced over at the blond bartender, studied him, and let my emotional shields down for just a second.

That was a mistake. So many emotions slammed into me. Anger, jealousy, and self-hatred coming from the trio of women behind me. Love and comfort from Ginger and Amos. And so much pain from Puck.

I slammed my walls back up just as my knees started to buckle. Puck cursed, dropping his knife onto the cutting board as he dashed forward to keep me from stumbling. "Shit, Birdie. Are you okay?"

I righted myself quickly, the pain from the emotions easing a fraction. But all I could think about was the inky blackness writhing around in Puck—a darkness that was the opposite of the façade he put on for the world. Words slipped from my mouth before I could stop them. "What happened to you?"

CHAPTER EIGHTEEN

Puck

I muttered a curse under my breath as I let go of Wren's elbow. My palm still burned from where it'd made contact. It was as if the echo of that touch had a heartbeat. It thumped within my palm like a living, breathing thing.

"Did you hit your head?" I asked, forcing humor into my voice.

It was a prick move, denying what Wren had somehow seen. But I didn't have a choice. I wasn't about to open up to her about all my wounds and scars. It was why I didn't usually let women into that circle of trust. Which made it all the more confusing why I wanted Wren there.

She took a step back, shaking herself out of whatever stupor she'd been in. "Sorry. It's none of my business."

"Birdie—"

"Do you want to make the princess her club soda or what?" Wren cut me off as she dumped ice into all three tall glasses.

Fuck.

This wasn't what I'd meant to do. But maybe it was for the best. Fucking things up meant creating a little distance so I could get my head on straight.

My wolf let out a snarl at the thought, letting me know how he felt about that plan. *Hell.* If my wolf wanted Wren close, I wouldn't have a choice. And as much as I would've liked to believe Ender's theory about Wren being here to destroy us all, it felt...wrong.

The same way Wren's scent was wrong yet equally alluring. I pulled it into my lungs now, trying to use it to calm my wolf. It worked, but the bell rang before I could get out another word.

"Order up."

"You tackle the drinks. I'll get Locke's lunch." Wren was gone before I could agree or disagree.

I glared down at my cutting board, annoyed that Locke, the lucky bastard, was getting Wren's attention. I went to work filling the Cokes, but when I got to the club soda, I was tempted to put jalapeños in it just to teach Cressida a lesson. I'd thought I made it clear that she and I weren't going to happen, but apparently, that needed reinforcement.

I watched Wren effortlessly weave through the tables. She moved like a dancer full of grace, power and ease all in one potent package. As she slid the plate in front of Locke, he said something that made her laugh.

A wave of jealousy nearly stole my breath. *Since when do I get jealous?* My brothers and I shared women on a regular basis, and I'd never felt even a flicker.

Worry niggled. The fear that Wren could be a potential mate. But I reminded myself that I'd just touched her and felt no mating bond. I'd only felt the pull of attraction. She might be a potential mate, but she wasn't a connection I'd be forced into. I still had my freedom.

I grabbed all three drinks and headed over to Cressida and her friends, placing the Cokes and her club soda on the table. "Cress, don't pull that shit again."

Her green eyes flared in surprise. "Puck—"

"I mean it. You're welcome here, but that doesn't mean you get to come in and play games. I told you it wasn't going to happen again. Tried to be nice about it. But apparently, that wasn't the play. It's *never* going to happen again. And if you pull any more bullshit power moves with my staff, I'll eighty-six your ass."

Her jaw dropped open into a tiny O full of shock, but I didn't wait for her to say anything. I just stalked away. The whole exchange had put me in a foul mood, and I knew I needed a run—in my wolf form. That always set me straight. But I wouldn't have that option until late tonight.

"You okay?" Locke's words gently prodded into my mind.

Our pack link allowed us to mind-speak with one another, but we didn't make a habit of using it unnecessarily. There were too many ways it could expose our otherworldly gifts.

"Fine."

"Puck, you can do many things but acting isn't one of them."

"Cressida's annoying," I finally admitted.

Locke let out a scoffing sound in my mind. *"You're just figuring that out?"*

"Yeah, yeah. Eat your BLT and shut up."

I kept an eye on Wren as she checked out two tables and took orders from a group of tourists. But I didn't miss Cressida's constant glares. I knew Wren could take her easily, but it didn't stop me from being on edge.

"Got my drinks?" Wren asked, coming to the end of the bar.

I set the girls' refills on her tray. "Here you go."

"The fact that you haven't asked me to marry you in the past hour is kind of freaking me out."

My lips twitched. "Birdie, let's run off to Vegas. Elvis can link us for all eternity."

She snorted. "'Hound Dog' does kind of seem like an appropriate theme song for you."

I let out a mock gasp and placed a hand on my chest. "Wren Delilah Archibald, how dare you?"

"That's not my name, Casanova."

I grinned at her. "I had to think up something on the fly." And I couldn't exactly admit that Locke had already run checks on the name she'd put on her rental agreement. Wren Harris—a person who didn't actually exist.

"And you went with Archibald?"

"What's wrong with Archibald?" I challenged.

Wren shook her head as she walked away. "You Brits are weird."

"You mean adorable, right?"

Wren wove through the tables, checking on patrons as she made her way to Cressida's group. When she got there, she deposited the two diets, but as she moved to grab the club soda, Cressida knocked the tray into her. Cressida tried to pretend it was an accident, but it was clear as day that she'd meant to do it.

Club soda drenched the front of Wren's tee. Under normal circumstances, I might've commented about being grateful for the wet T-shirt contest, but I was too livid to find any humor in the situation.

I stalked around the bar just as Cressida looked up at Wren in fake apology. "I'm so sorry. I'm just the clumsiest."

"No, what you are is a bitch," I snarled.

Cressida gasped as her two friends paled. "Puck, it was an accident."

"The hell it was. And I warned you. You pull bullshit again, and you're gone. Congrats, you're all banned."

This time, her friends gasped. "Puck, don't," Dara begged. "You guys have the best cheeseburgers in town."

"And are the only real bar within a thirty-mile radius," Siena whined.

"Should've thought about that before you became friends with a snake," I snapped.

"Puck, it's fine," Wren said, but I didn't miss the slight tremble in her voice. It wasn't fear, it was fury.

"The hell it is." I turned to Cressida. "Leave. Now."

She jutted out her chin. "We haven't finished eating."

"Too bad. Out, or I call the cops. You want to apologize and mean it? Maybe I'll reconsider."

"Come on, Cress," Siena whispered, grabbing her purse, her cheeks reddening.

Cressida glared at me as she shoved her chair back. "You'll regret this, Puck."

"Doubt it," I muttered.

The trio of women scurried out of the bar, and another customer started clapping. I turned slowly, taking in Wren. Her Arcane tee was soaking wet, and she held her tray in front of herself like some sort of shield.

Fuck.

"You realize this is a mess of your making."

I sent Locke a glare over my shoulder and then turned back to Wren. "Come on, I've got extra shirts in the office. Locke, you're on duty."

"Uh, you know that's gonna be a disaster, right?" he called after me. I just flipped him the bird in answer.

I guided Wren down the hallway but was careful not to touch her, remembering the incident the first day we met. My back teeth ground together, and anger at myself surged. I opened the door and gestured her inside.

Wren's brow furrowed. "Won't Dina be pissed that you're making yourself at home in her office?"

A chuckle slipped free, the sound taking me by surprise. "It's my office, Birdie."

This time, her nose scrunched, the move incredibly adorable. "Your office..."

"Arcane is my bar." I crossed to a sideboard, opened one of the cabinets, and grabbed a tee.

Wren's mouth opened and closed, then opened again before any words came out. "Why didn't you tell me?"

I shrugged and handed her the shirt. "You didn't ask."

She snatched it from my grasp, dropping her tray onto the couch along the wall. "Turn around," she ordered.

"Bossy little thing. I like it."

Wren sent me a pointed stare, and I held up both hands, doing as she instructed. I stared at the wall for a long moment, focusing on the painting hanging there. It was a play on that ridiculous dogs-playing-poker image, but instead of dogs, it was wolves.

I cleared my throat. "I'm sorry. That never should've happened."

Wren sighed. "Her actions aren't on you. I might question your romantic choices, but..."

I scoffed and ran a hand through my hair, tugging on the strands. "Trust me, nothing about that was romantic."

"I shouldn't judge. A little hate sex can be a good release."

Those words coming from her lips were so shocking that my gaze automatically moved over my shoulder. Wren was facing away from me, pulling the T-shirt over her head, but her back was completely on display.

A back riddled with scars. Different sizes and depths. Various stages of healing.

She'd been beaten. Tortured. Over and over again.

And I could only think one thing...

I was going to kill whoever had done it. And the death would not be quick.

CHAPTER NINETEEN

Wren

"OKAY, YOUR VIRGIN EYES ARE SAFE," I SAID, HUMOR lacing my tone. But there was no answer. "Puck?"

I turned around to find him glaring into space. "Buddy, are you reliving your last hate-sex escapade or something?"

That shook him out of whatever stupor he was in, and his face screwed up. "Did you just call me *buddy*?"

I fought a smile. "What's wrong with buddy?"

Puck let out a disgusted sound. "I am not a *buddy*."

I couldn't help the laugh that bubbled out of me. "What would you like to be called?"

He pondered that for a moment. "Sex god?"

"I don't think I'll be yelling that across the bar."

"Bummer." Shadows passed over Puck's green eyes, making the irises take on an emerald hue. "Are you okay, Birdie?"

I frowned, really taking him in. The question seemed to

encompass more than just me getting doused with Cressida's stupid club soda, but I couldn't figure it out. "Yeah, I'm fine. Why?"

Puck shook his head as if rethinking his approach. "I just—you shouldn't have to deal with that bullshit. *No one* has the right to mistreat you."

The back of my throat burned as if acid had been poured down it. I swallowed hard, trying to clear away the sting. It had been so long since anyone cared if I was mistreated or gave one damn whether I lived or died.

Pressure built in my chest, but I did my best not to give that away and let Puck know how much his words meant to me. "Romeo, if you haven't noticed, I can take pretty good care of myself."

There was no flicker of amusement in Puck's expression like I'd hoped. He just kept staring at me, so much emotion in those green eyes. "Even if you can, it's sometimes nice to know someone has your back. And I've got yours, Birdie."

The pressure intensified, almost brutal in its force. "Puck," I croaked.

"I'm kinda partial to Romeo. It's a hell of a lot better than fuckin' *buddy*."

That had a snort-laugh bubbling out of me. I grinned at him. "Sorry, buddy."

"Birdie," he growled.

With that, I knew I'd be calling him *buddy* for the foreseeable future. "Come on. We should get back out there."

Puck muttered a curse. "It'll be a miracle if Locke hasn't burned the place down by now."

I grinned, grabbed my tray, and hung my wet T-shirt on a coat rack before leaving the office. The low din from the bar told me there'd been an increase in patrons since we'd entered the office. When we reached the end of the hallway, Locke looked up from a sea of tables, panic written all over his face. "Help?"

A laugh bubbled out of me. Gods, he was adorable. I hurried over to him, where he held his phone, tapping in an order. "I don't think Gary's going to take orders from a phone."

"Right," Locke muttered, wincing.

"Don't worry. I've got it." I quickly jotted the list of orders onto my page, reading them off to the patrons as I did to confirm I had everything right.

"Thanks," Locke mumbled. "People-y things aren't really my strong suit."

I so got that. I reached out and squeezed his arm. "You're doing great. Why don't you take this to the kitchen, and I'll grab the other orders?"

He nodded, sending a lock of hair over his eyes. "Are you, um, are you okay? I'm sorry about Cressida."

I smiled reassuringly. "All good. Thankfully, it was just club soda and not anything sticky."

"Yeah, that's good. And everything with Puck? That's okay?" Locke's gaze flicked behind the bar, where Puck was filling drinks. He had a carefree smile on his face, but it was completely false. A lie. And it felt as if Locke could read that, too.

What the hell happened in that office?

"I think we're good," I said, pulling one corner of my mouth into a smile. "Well, other than the fact that he apparently really doesn't like being called *buddy*."

Locke barked out a laugh. "Wren. I would've paid good money to see you call him that."

"What did I do?" I asked with mock innocence.

"It's good for Puck. Keeps his ego in check."

I laughed, and the release of pressure felt damn good. "I'll do my best."

Locke shifted from one foot to the other, seeming to search for the words he wanted. Finally, he forced his gaze to mine and held it for almost a beat of five—longer than he ever had before.

"I'm glad you're okay." With that, he headed for the kitchen, the order sheet in hand.

I just blinked after him, wondering what the hell was going on. I'd only known these wolves for a matter of days, yet they made me feel more cared for than I'd felt in over a decade.

CHAPTER TWENTY

Kingston

THE KICK HIT ME IN THE SIDE WITH BRUTAL FORCE, BUT I welcomed the contact. I didn't wait to answer with a hit of my own, my gloved fist landing on Brix's rib cage. He let out a hiss, but I knew he felt the same relief and release I did, only for different reasons.

The only touch Brix could handle was the painful kind—sparring or the bite of a tattoo gun. But I guessed that was what happened when your entire family was murdered, and you were almost killed along with them. It twisted your mind.

The most *comfort* Brix could handle was from pack runs or sparring like this. And we gave him that. Let him be whoever he needed to be.

Brix tried to level a blow to my jaw, but I was too quick. I ducked, using his momentum to take him to the mat. In a matter of seconds, I had him in an armbar. He snarled in frustration but finally tapped out.

I sprang to my feet but didn't offer him a hand. I knew he wouldn't take it. Brix pushed up and extended his gloved hands. We tapped knuckles where the material covered our skin.

"You're looking sharp," I said, depositing my mouthguard in its case and grabbing my water.

Brix did the same, taking the bottle Ender offered. "Need to be. I've got a feeling this mage business isn't over."

A twitchy feeling skated over my skin, making me feel like I needed to spar all over again. Because my gut was screaming the same thing.

Crescent Kingdom Security worked many different jobs, which was why we'd become known as mercenaries. People thought we'd do anything for a price, but that wasn't true. We were very selective about the cases we took, and it was usually in a pattern: one for the bank account, and one for us—to make the world a better place.

This last job had been to keep us rolling in the green. But it didn't hurt that the dark mage coven we'd broken up had been up to some seriously fucked-up shit—human sacrifice fucked up. They had an entire network created to sell their dark services and products.

It took us weeks to infiltrate, and even when we did, we couldn't get them all. We simply didn't have the manpower. But we'd gotten enough to destroy their network paths. Even if they did rebuild, it would take years, and we had people in place who'd be watching so we could step in again if necessary.

Ender shoved off the side of the ring. "Has Locke picked up any movement?"

I shook my head, ducking between the ropes and climbing down. "Nothing."

"It's too quiet," Brix ground out.

Ender and I shared a look. He might be right, but we also knew that Brix being on edge wasn't good for anyone.

"You need an ink session?" Ender asked.

Ender was the only one Brix trusted to do his tattoo work. And those sessions were one of the few things that helped keep him in check.

Brix's jaw worked back and forth. "No."

Alrighty, then.

Before I could suggest going on a pack run, the gym doors swung open, revealing a seriously pissed-off Puck and a confused Locke trailing behind him. Puck's expression instantly had me on alert. "What happened?"

I knew if it were something seriously dire, he would've reached out through our mind link, but the fact that he looked this angry set my wolf on edge.

Puck quickly glanced around the gym. There were only a handful of people present. Still, he dipped his voice low. "It's Wren. She has scars all over her back. Like someone beat her, tortured her repeatedly."

A series of growls lit the air, mine included. Fury pulsed through me so fast and fierce that my nails lengthened into claws.

One of the guys on the treadmills glanced in our direction, the growls clearly making it to his ears. Even Clyde, whose hearing was shit, looked around for the source of the sound from his spot at the punching bags.

"Quiet," I ordered through our mind link. *"I don't think any of us wants the gym to know what we are."*

I watched as each of the guys tried to battle their beasts into submission, everyone but Ender, who simply had an annoyed look on his face. It was clear that we all felt a pull toward Wren, even him, despite his accusations against her. We all felt protective. She might not be our fated mate, but maybe, somehow, she was still destined to be ours.

I looked at Puck and dropped my voice even more. "Tell us what happened."

His back teeth ground together as he struggled for control.

"Cressida and her friends came into Arcane. Cress was a bitch to Wren."

"Shocker," Ender muttered. He had no patience for games like that. The ones he preferred were darker.

Puck cast him a look that would've had most men pissing themselves, but Ender just grinned at him. Puck turned back to me. "Cress spilled a drink on Wren, so I took her to my office to get her a dry shirt."

"Dry shirt, my ass," Ender clipped.

Puck charged him this time, but I was quicker, using my slight alpha edge to grab Puck's shirt and haul him back. "Don't," I ground out.

Puck's nostrils flared. "Get him under control, or I will give him a few new piercings."

My gaze met Ender's. "Enough. You aren't helping the situation."

A muscle in his jaw fluttered, but his head dipped a fraction, a sign of submission and acquiescence.

I slowly released my hold on Puck's shirt, waiting to make sure he didn't go for Ender again. I wouldn't have blamed him if he had.

Puck rolled his shoulders back, trying to release tension, but nothing seemed to loosen the muscles. "When she was changing into the fresh shirt, I saw her back for a second."

Ender let out a sound, but Brix elbowed him hard in the gut, shutting him right up.

Pain streaked across Puck's eyes. "There were too many to count. Scars from cuts, whips, burns."

"Maybe that's what she's into," Ender cut in. "Maybe she gets off on it."

One second, he was standing there. The next, Brix's fist collided with his nose in a satisfying crunch. We all moved instantly. I grabbed Brix's tee, careful not to touch him in any way, and tugged him back while Locke and Puck grabbed Ender.

"What the fuck? You broke my goddamn nose," Ender yelled, but his voice was garbled.

"You deserve worse," Brix snarled.

"Breathe," I ordered. "I'll deal with him."

Ender's eyes widened as I stalked toward him. "I was just pointing out a possibility."

"The hell you were. I know you don't trust a soul other than the four of us, and that's your choice. But I won't let you poison the reputation of a good woman just because you don't like her."

Ender gritted his teeth. "You don't know she's good."

But I did. I couldn't explain it, but I knew it in my bones. It was the same way I trusted my pack. "I do. And you won't disparage her in front of me."

My hand lashed out, fingers gripping Ender's nose. "Hold still." I snapped his nose back into place, and he let out a howl of pain. "Wouldn't want to risk your pretty face by letting it set crooked."

I knew we were getting looks now. I was sure the few fighters in the space thought we had completely lost it, but I couldn't find it in me to care. "Get him some ice," I ordered Brix.

He scowled but stalked off toward the machine. Puck snagged a towel from the ropes and tossed it to Ender. "Clean yourself up. You're bleeding everywhere."

Ender scowled at him but took the towel, gently dabbing at his nose. The bones and cartilage would heal in a matter of hours, but it would still probably hurt like hell for the next thirty minutes or so.

"Did she share anything about what or who might've caused the injuries?" I asked Puck.

He shook his head. "I didn't let on that I saw them. Didn't want to make her uncomfortable or scare her into bolting."

"Smart play. We need to hope she'll open up with time. I can't think of any other way to find out what she's running from," I said, squeezing the back of my neck.

"I could find out," Ender said sulkily.

My gaze zeroed in on the assassin. There was a reason he was known as The Archer outside of the fact that his weapon of choice was bow and arrow. He was the kind of killer who stalked his prey for weeks before ending their lives. They never knew they were in the crosshairs until it was too late.

"Ender," Puck growled.

"I won't kill her," he snapped. But he sounded like not killing Wren was the equivalent of getting coal in his stocking on Christmas Day.

I sighed. "I don't know if that's a good idea."

"Do you have a better one?" Ender challenged. "Web boy came up with zilch."

Locke glared at him. "Remember this the next time you're begging me to hack more Candy Crush lives for you."

Ender winced, realizing his misstep. Locke could destroy any of our lives with just a few keystrokes.

"Here," Brix said, throwing a bag of ice at Ender.

End caught it one-handed but scowled. "I just meant that following her might give us the answers we need."

"Stalking her, you mean," Puck accused.

"Potato, poh-tah-toh," Ender said, pressing the ice to his nose with a wince. "Shit, Brix. Did you get metal injected into your knuckles or something?"

Brix extended his hands, examining them. "No, but that's not a bad idea."

Jesus.

"Don't do it," Locke said, his voice low. "If she finds out any of us is tracking her, she's gone." His gaze dipped to the floor. "I don't want her to leave."

Just thinking about the possibility had an ache taking root in my chest. I didn't want that either.

Footsteps sounded, making us all look up. There was the woman of the hour. She looked just as beautiful as ever. Her dark hair hung around her face in loose waves, and her olive-toned skin only made those turquoise eyes stand out more. Even the scar on her face somehow managed to look beautiful.

Wren's gaze moved to Ender, her eyes flaring. "What the hell happened to you? Did a priest try to exorcise the devil out of you?" She held up two fingers in a makeshift cross. "I just say no to projectile green puke."

CHAPTER TWENTY-ONE

Wren

THE GUYS ALL LOOKED AT ME LIKE I'D GROWN TWO HEADS. Maybe they weren't up on their *Exorcist* references. But hell, Ender looked like he'd gone a round with Mike Tyson.

Then Puck started laughing, and Kingston joined in. I thought I might've even heard a chuckle from Brix. But it was Locke who came through for me. "It does seem like an excellent day for an exorcism."

I grinned at him, my smile huge. "I knew you were my favorite."

"Hey," Puck complained. "I thought *I* was your favorite."

"Not today, buddy. It's Locke all the way."

Puck's face transformed into a scowl. "Birdie…"

I couldn't help but laugh, but it died as I turned to find Brix studying me like some sort of specimen on a lab slide. This was it. The moment that could make or break things. "Sorry I freaked the other day. Not sure if you guys know this, but you kind of have an awful reputation."

Kingston's lips twitched. "Awful?"

"You're called The Diablos. That doesn't exactly bring up mental images of kittens and puppies."

King groaned. "That's not what we call ourselves. We like to go by the Arcane Pack."

I lifted a brow in challenge. "I heard you were some crazy group of mercenaries."

Puck grinned. "I like being known as a mercenary."

"You would, buddy."

He just growled at me.

"We are a security firm," Kingston explained. "We take jobs on a case-by-case basis. One of them was dismantling a cartel in Mexico. *They* called us The Diablos. I guess it stuck in certain circles."

Interesting. I wondered how much of that was true. I knew we were leaving out one very important fact: They were shifters. So, they had senses and gifts that gave them an edge against human factions like a cartel. But I knew they had to face supernatural foes, as well.

"I guess I'd be okay with it if a drug cartel called me the devil," I mumbled.

Kingston's lips twitched. "Great point."

Brix moved in closer, and I swore I heard him sniffing me. I stiffened. My scent shields, the ones that kept my wolf and caster scents hidden, had become second nature by now. They only slipped when I went into an especially deep sleep. But I did a mental check just to be sure. All in place.

I turned to Brix, sending him a megawatt smile, something that seemed to confuse him. "If I smell like fried food, blame buddy over there." I gestured at Puck. "He refused to help me with the tables."

"Way to throw me under the bus, Birdie," Puck grumbled.

Brix studied me, his head tilting from one side to the other. The move was animalistic in nature, maybe because he was closer to his beast than the rest of them. It was always a delicate balance between human and animal. Sometimes, the animal won.

"You smell…wrong," Brix said, a growl bleeding into his voice.

"All right, then," Puck interjected, throwing a towel at his friend. "That's no way to talk to a lady. It's time for you to get in your weight training."

"I need to get my workout in, too," I muttered, heading toward the treadmills. But a chill skittered over my spine. I couldn't help but wonder what Brix scented that I couldn't.

"Girlie, you planning on taking on a heavyweight champ I don't know about?" Clyde asked as he came up beside the speed bag.

I didn't let his distraction ruin my rhythm. "Just working out the day's stressors."

"Heard some gals were mean to you at the bar. Need me to have a word?"

I slowed my tempo on the bag as warmth spread through me. "I'm good. I think they'll be too embarrassed to show their faces for a while."

"Good," Clyde harrumphed.

I stepped back from the bag, unwinding my wraps. "Don't gotta worry about me."

"Just because I know you can handle yourself doesn't mean I don't worry," he mumbled.

I grinned at him. "I appreciate it."

Clyde swung his keys around his finger. "I'm headin' out. King's locking up tonight," he said as if checking if that was okay.

Unease slid through me. Brix's scent comment had me tweaked, as did the fact that all five wolves had hung around throughout my evening workout. Some did their own workouts, King did some training, and Locke holed up on the couch, fingers flying across his keyboard.

But I'd powered through. I wouldn't give The Diablos any reason to suspect that something was up. I shot Clyde another smile. "Sounds good. I want to work on some grappling this week."

That had him returning my grin. "You got it, girlie. See you."

"See ya, gramps."

He chuckled as he headed for the door while I moved for my bag near the back wall. I tossed my wraps into it and grabbed a towel from one of the stacks in the corner. I wanted to bail so badly, but I wasn't changing my routine. Would do nothing that gave me away.

I took my time going through my stretches, forcing myself to whisper the counts aloud so I didn't rush. By the time I was finished, all the guys appeared to be wrapping up. I wasn't sure that was a coincidence.

Tossing the towel into a hamper, I grabbed my bag and headed toward the door. Puck jogged to catch up with me, grabbing the handle before I could. "Leaving without saying goodbye? Why are you trying to break my heart?"

I patted his chest. "I think you'll survive, buddy."

"I like watching that vein in his temple pulse when you call him that," Locke said, laughter in his voice.

A little of the tension thrumming through me eased at the banter. I felt the most comfortable with Puck and Locke. Something about them was a little less intense than the other three.

"Hurry up," Ender complained. "I'm fucking starving."

"Wouldn't want your sensitive Sally to get hangry," I singsonged. "Better get him home."

Kingston chuckled, clapping Ender on the shoulder as we stepped outside. "She knows you too well."

The parking lot seemed darker than usual, and I found my gaze searching out the reason. One of the pole lights was out. I frowned. Something about that did not sit well with me.

And then I scented it.

Sulfur. The scent that always accompanied dark magic.

Fuck.

My gaze instantly went to the tree line. That's when I saw them—at least a dozen, all wearing dark robes, their faces nothing but shadows.

One raised their hands in a casting motion, and I felt my magic rise in response. But all I could think about was that I had to warn the wolves.

"Watch out!" I screamed.

And then, all the remaining lights in the parking lot shattered.

CHAPTER TWENTY-TWO

Wren

Kingston instantly began barking orders at the rest of the guys, but my focus was entirely on the dark mages. Their magic was just as their name suggested, pulling from the shadows. It had a cost—the kind that meant loss of life.

It was in complete opposition to my caster half. Casters got their power from nature and the world around them. The elements and life fed us.

I'd learned all I could about my mother's side, but there was only so much I could gather without learning from another caster. And that was too risky.

Still, I ducked my head and whispered an incantation as one of the robed figures raised their hand, a ball of smoky evil in their palm. Sweat broke out on my brow. Holding my shields in place and trying to cast a protection spell was almost more than my body could handle.

"Wren," Kingston clipped. "Get back in the gym."

"Are you out of your mind?" I shot back. "There are more than twelve of them and only five of you."

"You don't know what you're up against, Little Warrior."

My back teeth ground together. "Maybe not, but I can still help." The *maybe* was the only thing that kept my words from being an outright lie.

"Birdie, get your cute ass in the gym," Puck called, pulling two guns from his duffel.

The dark mage laughed and threw his ball of smoke in Puck's direction. Puck ducked, but the smoke hit my protection ward and stopped there. All the guys stared.

"What. The. Hell. Was. That?" Ender snarled.

I glanced at him, taking in the fact that he now held what looked like a bow and arrow. I frowned, confused, but quickly turned as the dark mage snarled in fury.

"Your magic is no match for mine." The dark mage's hood slipped back as he raised his hand, revealing skin so pale it was almost translucent and eyes that were pure white.

The hand raise was an order, and all the mages charged.

"Ender. Roof," Kingston yelled.

Ender shot something toward the roof that pulled him with it. Before long, he was slinging arrows at the mages. I had to give it to them, they were fast. They dodged and wove, blocking with blades and magic.

That's when I saw them. It wasn't a dozen-plus dark mages—it was at least twice that many. *Holy hell.* They moved on us in a wave.

Puck took shot after shot, but the bullets simply bounced off the creatures like nothing. He cursed. "They have a protection spell in place. It has to be hand-to-hand. A blade to the throat or the heart."

Brix tossed a duffel into the center of the parking lot, and I dashed forward, taking a dagger. I'd done a fair amount of weapons training, but blades weren't exactly my forte. I shot Brix a look. "Just like a Boy Scout. Always be prepared."

I swore I saw the hint of a smile on his lips right before Locke shouted, "Wren, behind you."

I whirled, the blade raised. I blocked the blow the dark mage leveled on me, his eyes glowing in fury. My knee came up between his legs, and he howled in pain. I didn't miss my chance. While he was distracted, I slid my blade across his throat.

The gurgling sound had bile churning in my stomach, but it wasn't red blood that appeared. It was a sticky black substance. The kind that showed just how evil the mage was. The more lives they took, the darker their blood became.

I shoved the mage back with a kick, sending him crashing into another. Movement caught my eye as Ender sailed down into the fray. He moved with effortless grace, executing a spin that cost three mages their heads. It should've been the furthest thing from beauty, but it somehow wasn't. It was art in its own right.

A snarl sounded to my left, and I lifted my dagger in defense. The mage's head cocked. "Wrong," he whispered, his voice almost garbled.

My skin bristled as I felt something pressing against my shields. The dark mage was trying to get into my mind. *Oh, hell no.*

My body twisted, and I put all my strength into a side kick, sending the mage stumbling back a few steps. He cocked his head again. "Strong," he rasped.

There was almost a grudging respect in the word as he lifted his sword. "What. Are. You?"

I was suddenly grateful that the guys were too busy to hear the mage's words. Locke was taking on two robed figures, moving in a way that told me he was no stranger to fighting, even if he did spend most of his time behind a computer screen. Kingston fought three mages using a combination of blade and fists. Two lay dead at his feet.

Puck had what looked like a katana sword, and as he spun, he took the head clean off of one of the mages. Brix fought silently, a blade in each hand, wielding them as if they were an extension of his fingers. And Ender had found a way to use his bow again. He shot an arrow point-blank into a mage's heart, sending him crumpling to the ground.

My adversary prowled forward, his mental attack back in full force. I nearly stumbled as an invisible ice pick jammed into my head. I shoved it back with all my might, charging forward.

My blade sliced at the mage. He let out a piercing scream of pain but didn't let it stop him. He lashed out with a blow to my temple, stunning me. Then, a kick sent my blade flying.

The mage raised his sword, and I braced for the pain. But an arrow came from out of nowhere, piercing the mage's shoulder. He yowled, whispered an incantation, and then disappeared into a puff of black smoke.

I didn't have time to thank Ender or wonder why the hell he was watching my back when I was pretty sure he'd rather see me dead. I dove toward my blade just as Kingston shouted.

"Puck! Behind you!"

It was as if it happened in slow-motion snapshots. I took in Puck and the two mages he was fighting in front of him, then the mage approaching from the back, sword at the ready. I didn't think, I simply lunged between the mage and Puck.

I tried to block the blow, but I wasn't quite fast enough. The sword pierced my side, sending white-hot pain coursing through me. Spots danced in front of my vision. So much pain.

I heard a shout, and then Brix's furious face filled my vision. His knife sliced across the mage's throat, but it was too late. I was already fading. My eyesight tunneling. And then, I was falling.

CHAPTER TWENTY-THREE

Brix

I SLICED MY BLADE ACROSS THE MAGE'S THROAT, EVIL SPILLING from his jugular. There was no satisfaction. No feeling.

I only had eyes for Wren.

King had been right to name her Little Warrior. She was tiny but so incredibly fierce. So much so that she hadn't hesitated to dive in front of a sword to protect Puck.

The mage crumpled to the ground, his blade falling with him. But the damage had been done. Wren clutched her side, her eyes going wide as blood seeped through her fingers. A deep red. So alive. Not the evil the dark mages carried inside them.

Wren stumbled, and I didn't hesitate. I lurched forward, dropping my knives to the ground so I could help her. I caught her easily, and a moan slipped from her lips. "We need to move," I snarled.

Locke let loose a stream of curses. "Getting the SUV." He jammed a knife into a mage's heart and then took off running across the parking lot. Locke hated fighting. It wasn't in his nature. But he did it for us. And maybe for Wren.

I pressed my hand to her wound, knowing I needed to keep pressure on it. Humans were so weak. Delicate. Breakable.

"Fuck," Puck cursed. "Why did she do that?" Panic scorched his eyes, but he kept right on fighting, slaying as many mages as he could.

I stared down at Wren's face. The scar that ran from her forehead to her jaw, just missing her eye, stood out even more now with how pale she was. I had the bizarre urge to trace it with my finger. That wasn't me. I didn't touch people if I could avoid it.

When I did, the panic set in like hundreds of snakes constricting my chest, neck, and limbs. But here I was, holding Wren with no such feelings. Maybe because I knew she was no threat to me. Something told me that was a lie.

Tires screeched, and two mages dove out of Locke's way as he gunned the engine. He brought the blacked-out SUV to a skidding halt in front of me and jumped out. "Oh, gods," he whispered.

His worry was evident in his tone. I knew that's what I *should* be feeling, but I didn't have those normal human emotions. I simply felt *uncomfortable*—or the fiery heat of what should've been rage.

"Create a circle," Kingston yelled. "Get her into the SUV."

My brothers created a crescent moon of protection around us. Puck, King, and Ender fought off as many of the mages as they could, and I pushed to my feet, cradling Wren in my arms. She moaned, not fully unconscious but close.

Locke opened the door to the back seat, and I slid inside with Wren still cradled against me. She shifted as if trying to alleviate her pain, and I felt a prickle of *something* in my chest—a pins-and-needles sensation like your fingers waking up after being asleep for hours.

What was that?

Shouts sounded outside as Locke slid behind the wheel. Kingston and Puck filed in beside me while Ender ran around to the front passenger seat. The moment he was in the SUV, Locke gunned the engine and took off across the parking lot. He instantly moved into an evasive maneuver that would disguise our route if any mages followed.

Our compound had magical protections, ones we'd paid a caster a pretty penny to implement. The wards they had created prevented any spells from finding our home and any supernaturals with ill intent from crossing our borders. But the moment we stepped outside, we were fair game.

"Faster," Puck ground out, sending a worried glance in Wren's direction. "She's not looking so good."

As if agreeing, Wren let out another soft moan.

"She'll be fine," King clipped as if she were a subordinate forced to follow his orders and there was no other choice.

Still, Locke pressed down on the accelerator. "Open the gate." His voice was quiet like always, but there was an underlying fury there I'd never heard from him before.

Ender pulled out his phone and tapped on the screen, but he didn't say a word. He would usually be breaking down the fight and outlining our next steps. But not now. It was as if he was still trying to make sense of it all.

Gravel spit under the SUV's tires as Locke hit our property line. I should've felt some sort of ease at being within the wards, but I didn't.

It took less than five minutes to reach the house we'd had built almost a decade ago. The dark wood was almost black, punctuated by accents of more natural wood in a few strategic places. The structure was massive, but we were five shifters, and all liked our space.

The SUV screeched to a halt, and everyone but Wren and I were out in an instant. Ender yanked open the door, and I slid out, still cradling her in my arms. Locke had already run ahead to open the front door.

"Get her to medical," King clipped.

Normally, I would've rolled my eyes at the idiotic order. It wasn't like I was taking her to the kitchen for a snack. But I didn't say anything, simply strode down the long hallway to the small room at the back of the house. It held all the medical supplies and healing potions we had on hand. But none of us had worked on a human before.

I laid Wren on a gurney as Kingston donned nitrile gloves. He had the most medical training thanks to owning the gym. "I need gauze, a suture kit, and hydrogen peroxide."

In a matter of seconds, the supplies were on the cart next to him. "Lift her shirt," he ordered.

I swallowed hard but gently lifted the ruined workout top. A snarl left my lips on instinct. It wasn't just the wound still oozing blood, it was the scars decorating her torso. Her skin was littered with them. Burns. Blade marks. What looked like damage from a whip.

Other growls lit the air, and the scent of fury swirled around us.

"Hold it together," King ground out. "We need to treat her."

"She's human. Shouldn't we take her to a hospital? What if she needs surgery?" Locke asked.

"And say what?" Ender challenged. "She got into a sword fight with a creature of dark magic and lost?"

"I don't know what," Locke shot back. "But I'm not about to let her die."

Something shifted in the air. A scent. It laced the fury as if coating it.

My jaw went slack as I stared down at Wren. The room went silent as we gawked at her unconscious form. It was *her* scent we smelled.

That same wildflowers and rain as before, but with a different root now. She smelled of wolf. *And* of caster.

But more than that, she smelled like...home.

CHAPTER TWENTY-FOUR

Wren

THE FEELING OF HEAT WOKE ME. THE UNCOMFORTABLE kind. The type that occurred when you'd piled too many blankets on the bed the night before.

My eyelids fluttered, bright light filling my vision with each brief blink. But something else filled my senses, teasing my nose, and it wasn't the scents of home. I smelled wolf—a mix of aromas I'd grown to know well over the past week.

My eyes flew open. Five males were perched around a room far nicer than anything I'd ever stayed in. It had a modern air to it—clean lines, nothing too crowded, with massive windows that looked out onto the surrounding forest. The art was tasteful, too—a modern take on landscapes with imperfect trees formed out of globs of paint.

Brix and Ender sat on a sofa pushed against the far wall, and Puck lounged in an overstuffed chair while Locke and Kingston perched on the end of the bed.

King's gaze ran over my face. "How do you feel?"

Memories came back to me in flashes. Snapshots of the fight, diving in front of the sword. My gaze snapped to Puck. "You're okay?"

He pushed up from his chair. "I'm fine, thanks to you. What the hell were you thinking?"

I bristled at his tone. "Trying to save your life. I've gotten used to your incessant chatter."

I expected someone in the group to laugh, but I didn't even get a chuckle. Worry slid through me, and I mentally checked my shields. Both the emotional and scent ones were in place.

"You shouldn't have done it," Puck ground out.

I sighed, wincing as I pushed up against the pillows. I could tell the wound was healing, but it wasn't quite there yet. I'd have to keep the guys from examining it. They'd have too many questions about my miraculous healing if they did.

"You've grown on me," I admitted. "I didn't want to see you get dead."

Puck stared at me for a long moment as if trying to pull all my secrets from my head. I fought the urge to squirm.

"Are you hungry?" Locke asked, cutting into the awkward silence. "I can go get you something—"

"She talks first," Ender snarled, shoving up from the couch. "You might be hiding your scent now, but we all smelled it. You're a wolf. A wolf *and* a fucking caster."

Hybrids were rare, and many pregnancies didn't take. Some were old school enough to believe hybrids were an abomination and should be wiped from the Earth. As Ender prowled toward the bed, I wondered if he was one of them.

King stood, giving Ender a shove. "Back off. She's just waking up."

"She's been lying to all of us," he growled. "And you just want to feed her tea and cookies?"

Shit. Shit. Shit.

My scent shields must've failed when I was unconscious. "I haven't lied to you." The words were out of my mouth before I could stop them.

Ender's amber eyes flashed gold. "You're doing it again now."

I jutted out my chin in defiance. "I'm sorry, did you ask me if I was a wolf? If I was a caster? I don't think you did."

His jaw worked back and forth, and anger flitted over his expression.

Puck clapped him on the shoulder. "She's got you there. We never asked."

A little relief slid through me at that, but I knew I was screwed. I knew my father had put a price on my head. He wanted me delivered back to him alive so he could torture me all over again. It seemed Ender would be more than happy to do it.

Kingston turned to me. "Why do you hide your true nature? Being a hybrid is nothing to be ashamed of."

I let out a huff of air. "Not everyone agrees with you. How could I know your pack's opinion on hybrids?"

I was hedging, and I knew it. It wasn't fair, but I didn't have any other choice. Besides, I'd become a master at half-truths and carefully dodged questions.

"Tell us about the scars."

The words came from the man farthest from me, the darkest of the bunch. The only light in him was his eyes, a blue-green swirling now as they locked on to me. But even with those hypnotizing colors…

The scars. Fucking hell.

I had no believable explanation. It was why I worked so hard to keep them covered.

Puck's brow furrowed as he looked down at me. "Are you running from the person who did it?"

My mouth clamped shut so hard my teeth nipped my bottom lip, the copper taste of blood filling my mouth.

Brix stood, his movements like a panther's as he prowled

toward me. "Your body is covered in scar tissue. Burns, cuts, whip marks."

I cringed, each word bringing forth a memory.

Those blue-green eyes narrowed on me, the knife tattooed next to one flexing with the movement. "Who. Did. This. To. You?"

It was as if the temperature in the room had dropped twenty degrees. Brix's fury didn't run to fire; it was like ice—and currently pointed directly at me.

It was too much to bear. My jaw loosened, my tongue moving before I could stop it as I gave him the only truth I could. "Evil incarnate."

CHAPTER TWENTY-FIVE

Locke

E*VIL INCARNATE.*”

Wren’s words echoed in my mind as my brothers argued in the kitchen. But I could only think of the woman lying in the guest room bed that never held guests because we never trusted anyone enough to let them across our borders.

It wasn’t just Wren’s words that held me hostage; it was how she’d said them. Devoid of all emotion. Like a robot.

That wasn’t the woman I’d been growing to know over the past week. She was fire and kindness, light and mirth, and I wanted to kill whoever had stolen that away.

“I want to burn them alive and feed their entrails to the buzzards,” Brix snarled.

Apparently, I wasn’t the only one who felt that way. Some of us were just a bit more colorful about it.

“Jesus,” Ender muttered. “Get a grip. We don’t even know if

she's telling us the truth. It could all be a cover story to garner sympathy."

Puck shoved him hard. "What the hell's wrong with you? No one would do that to themselves."

"Did. You. Just. Push. Me?" Ender clipped.

"Shut up!" I yelled. "All of you just shut the hell up. We're going to keep her safe. We're going to give her time to heal and not force her to talk about anything she doesn't want to. And if any of you try to push her, I'll hack your whole lives. You won't be able to move without hemorrhaging money or your phone *accidentally* sending out fart sounds."

Four sets of eyes came to me. Ender's and Puck's expressions were full of shock, interest filled Brix's, and I saw respect in Kingston's eyes.

"Did he just threaten us?" Puck asked, sounding more confused than anything.

I understood it. I'd never been a dominant wolf. It was why my parents had abandoned me as a pup. I'd been worth less than dirt to them.

But my brothers here? They saw my value, it just wasn't usually in fights or issuing threats.

"I think he did," King said, one corner of his mouth kicking up.

I was too annoyed to respond to either of them. I grabbed the tray I'd prepared for Wren and stalked toward her room. The anger and frustration were so strong in me that I forgot to even knock. Pushing into the room, I came up short.

Wren was trying desperately to get one of the huge picture windows open. At the sound of the door, she whirled, hands up in a defensive posture.

The move sent an ache through my chest. "I'm not going to hurt you. I'd never hurt you."

Wren's hands dropped a fraction. "I don't know, you seem pretty well trained."

My lips twitched as I set the tray on the bed, lowering myself to the bench at the foot of it. "I hate fighting."

She studied me for a moment before moving closer. "Why?"

"I'm sure you've sensed that I'm not exactly dominant." Wolves could sense those levels in one another; it was a self-defense technique.

She tugged the corner of her lip between her teeth. "I'm not either. It doesn't mean we can't learn."

My brows lifted at that. In the handful of moments I'd been able to inhale Wren's true scent, I hadn't felt her dominance or lack thereof. But I'd been too wrapped up in trying to figure out *what* she was.

"I've learned. I've mastered enough to keep myself safe. But I still don't like it," I admitted.

Wren lowered herself to the mattress. "Fair. The world would be a better place without all the bloodshed."

"I prefer to keep my battles to firewalls and system backdoors."

"You've got me there. I wish I were better at that sort of thing."

My wolf perked up at that, his ears twitching. "I could teach you."

The words were out of my mouth before I could stop them. It was monumentally stupid.

"Really?" Wren asked, something that sounded a lot like hope in her voice.

My gaze snuck up to her face for the briefest of moments. There was more than beauty there. There was genuine interest. "Sure. I don't have many people I can geek about tech with."

An adorable little furrow appeared between Wren's brows. "The rest of the guys don't like that stuff?"

One corner of my mouth kicked up. "They like the intel I provide, but none of them has enough patience to sit behind a monitor for hours." I shook my head. "Which doesn't even make any sense because Ender will lie in wait for days for his targets."

"Targets?" she asked.

I snapped my mouth closed. End wouldn't be happy I was spilling his secrets.

"Don't worry. You didn't let me in on anything I didn't already suspect. You guys have a pretty gnarly reputation in the supernatural world."

I shifted on the bench. I knew we had a rep, but it didn't mean I liked it. "We're trying to do good. Most of the time, anyway."

Wren was quiet for a moment. Then I watched as her slender fingers reached out to pluck a grape from the snack tray I'd made for her. The pleasure I got from her eating something I had brought her was ridiculous—being able to take care of her in some small way.

My gaze grew braver, inching up her body. Making eye contact wasn't something I'd ever been especially comfortable with, but I wanted to see Wren, at least as much of her as I could. My eyes tracked higher, watching her lips move as she chewed. The perfect berry pink.

"I know you helped my friend Hayden. I'm not sure if I'm supposed to know, but I do," Wren said quietly.

Her friend had ended up in the clutches of a seriously messed-up dragon shifter, and we'd been happy to deal out a little justice. My gaze darted up for the briefest of moments, just long enough to get a look at those turquoise eyes.

"Do they know about you? What you are?" I asked.

Wren stiffened, and I knew I was treading on thin ice. Still, she answered. "Yes. I asked them to keep my secret."

"Why?" I pressed. "Why do you hide your true nature? Having two supernatural sides is a gift."

Tension radiated through her jaw and down her neck. "It's complicated."

"Wren—"

"I'm getting pretty tired. You know how healing can take it out of you. I'm going back to sleep for a bit."

I knew when I'd been shut down. I'd give her this, her space. Time. "I'll never force you to talk about something you don't want to," I said softly as I stood. "I was only trying to understand."

But just because I wouldn't push didn't mean that I wouldn't do everything in my power to keep her safe.

CHAPTER TWENTY-SIX

Wren

Guilt swept through me, dark and heavy like oil spreading across a crystalline ocean. Forcing Locke out was like kicking a puppy. And he only made it worse by being so damn understanding.

I sighed, plucking a grape from the tray and popping it into my mouth. The flavors of it exploded on my tongue. Even the food was better here.

As I looked around the room again, it made sense. It was clear the guys had plenty of money for the best of everything. But that did nothing to calm my wolf.

She paced back and forth, feeling trapped being in this room. And something else had her on edge. Something that was making her snap and snarl, despite the fact that she loved being surrounded by these males' scents.

"All right," I muttered. "I'm looking for a way out."

I couldn't stay here. Not anymore. It was too risky.

Pushing to my feet, I felt a slight twinge in my side. But it was already ten times better than when I'd woken up. I knew I'd be back to 100 percent by tonight.

Scanning the room, I moved on from the picture window I'd had no luck with. This time, I went for a skinny pane I wasn't sure would open. My gaze ran along the seam until I came to a latch. I grinned until I saw the lock. It was one of those that was supposed to have a key in it, but this one was missing.

Damn, those wolves.

They might be taking care of me, but this was still a prison.

I lifted a hand to my hair, feeling around. My rubber band had come free at some point, but I sighed in relief when I found one of the bobby pins. Hiding things on my body that could be helpful in moments like these had become habit over the years.

Tugging the pin free, I bent it into a shape that I thought might do the trick and stretched up onto my tiptoes to place the hairpin into the lock. I maneuvered left, then right, trying to feel for the mechanisms. Just when it seemed like it might catch—

"Going somewhere, Little Warrior?" Brix asked, his voice raspy.

I whirled, turning to see the lot of them standing inside the bedroom, Brix leading the way. I let out a huff of air. "Make a little noise when you enter a room, would you? It's rude to sneak up on someone."

"It's rude to sneak out of someone's home after they saved your life," King shot back.

I scoffed. "I would've healed on my own."

His eyes narrowed on me. "Not if the wound got infected."

I let out a long sigh. "Thank you for taking care of me. But I need to get going."

Puck moved forward, breaking free of the group. "When you say *get going*, why do I have a feeling you don't just mean going back to your apartment?"

I winced. The truth was, I hated the idea of leaving. My wolf snarled and spat at the thought, grasping for the reins of control. I clamped down on her, not allowing the shift she so desperately wanted. I'd thought simply being in the vicinity of other wolves would help, but apparently, it wasn't enough. Not even close. She was still edging into feral territory.

"There's too much heat here. I need to keep moving," I admitted. I left out the part about me not trusting Ender not to sell me out to the highest bidder. And Bastian's cool million-dollar offer would be at the top of that list. I shuddered at the idea.

"You can't," Kingston clipped. "It's not safe."

"Let her go," Ender muttered. "For all we know, she's the one who tipped off the dark mages about our location."

My jaw dropped. I wouldn't even do that to *him* alone. Certainly not to the rest of the guys.

"Hey, shit for brains," Puck shot back. "Remember the part where she stepped in front of a sword for me? Doubt she'd do that if she was working for the dark mages."

Ender's jaw worked back and forth as his eyes started to glow. "She could've done it to ingratiate herself to us."

"Dude," I muttered. "You might have nice beds around here, but that isn't worth a sword to the gut."

A smile stretched across Puck's face. "You know, I have fifteen-hundred-thread-count sheets. I order them special from Italy. You might want to try those out before you bail."

Kingston smacked him upside the head, and Ender glared. "Not the time, Puck."

"Right. Thwarting runaway plans is more important," Puck mumbled.

My gaze found Locke's among them, the only one who hadn't said a word. Like usual, he only held my stare for a single beat, maybe two, but in that brief moment, I saw the hurt there. Hurt that had guilt springing back to life inside me.

"I appreciate everything you guys have done," I began. "It's not that I don't. I just—this is what's safest for me."

"They know what you are," Brix growled low. "The dark mages."

My gaze shot to him. "They don't. My scent shields didn't falter in that battle." Annoyance fluttered to the surface because this was a point of pride.

Brix prowled toward me, that panther-like grace in full effect. He stopped mere inches from me and inhaled deeply. His wolf flashed in his eyes, and I saw annoyance there. "They know you smelled *wrong*. And they know *someone* put up a shield to block their magic. How long do you think it will take for them to figure out it was you?"

My heart hammered against my ribs as the memory of the mage I'd fought flashed in my mind. *"What. Are. You?"* He'd known something was off about me.

"Is that the most you've ever heard Brix speak at once?" Puck whispered.

"Shut up," Locke hissed.

I straightened my spine. "All the more reason for me to leave."

"Birdie, they'll already have people watching the entrances and exits to town," Puck reasoned.

Hell.

I knew in my gut he was right. Knew leaving on my own right now would put me at risk. But so would staying. The dark mages would find me just as easily in my tiny apartment above Arcane.

My wolf raked her claws against her prison, demanding I free her to slay every one of those dark mages. But we would be no match for them.

"There's only one answer." King's voice rang out, alpha vibes bleeding into his tone. "You'll have to stay here."

CHAPTER TWENTY-SEVEN

Wren

I blinked at Kingston a few times. "I'm sorry, what did you say?"

"You'll need to stay here," he replied matter-of-factly as if his words weren't completely unhinged. "It's the only thing that makes sense."

"For you, maybe," Ender snarled. "All you care about is fucking her and picking up the pieces of whatever mess she's got herself caught up in."

I bristled at that, but Puck gave him a hard shove before I could say a word. "Do you want me to break your nose this time? Twice in forty-eight hours might be a new record."

"You can't tell me *you* actually think this is a good idea," Ender clipped. "We have a no-females rule in the compound for a reason."

I scoffed. "What is this? Second grade and a no-girls-allowed club?"

Ender skewered me with a look that should've had me

stumbling back a few steps, but I wasn't about to back down to this idiot. It didn't matter how good of a fighter he was.

"It's a no-traitors-allowed club," he snapped. "And you haven't proven yourself not to be one."

"These are extenuating circumstances, End," Kingston said, his voice calm. "She fought with us and saved Puck's life. She's earned our loyalty."

"If Puck was stupid enough to leave his back wide open, then he would have deserved whatever he got," Ender shot back.

The entire room went silent for a beat and then erupted. It wasn't Brix who decked Ender this time; it was Puck. And his fist connected with Ender's jaw, the force of it enough to send Ender's head snapping back. The guys yelled as they struggled to pull them apart.

Fiery claws raked at my emotional shields. They were already drained from the past forty-eight hours—heightened emotion tended to do that. Spots danced across my vision as I staggered back a step. It felt like tiny ice picks were jamming into my brain.

"What's wrong with her?" Locke's voice sounded far away.

Puck cursed. "She gets migraines." I heard shuffling as he ordered everyone out. "I'll get the tincture."

"Ice pack, too," Locke called, but he was already moving around the room, drawing the curtains closed and flicking off the lights.

"Leave one on," I croaked.

"You don't want total darkness?" Locke asked softly.

"No. Need one on. Just a little one." I couldn't have complete dark. It reminded me of the pit too much. And I couldn't go back there.

"Okay. I've got this one on right here." Locke chose a small lamp on the other side of the room. There was enough of a glow to know I wasn't back *there,* but not so much that it hurt my eyes.

"Thank you," I rasped.

"Come on," Locke said. "Let's get you back to bed." He pulled the covers back, moving the tray of food to the other side of the mattress.

I slid between the sheets, no fight left in me. The pain was too bad. Locke gently pulled the comforter back into place as I heard the door open.

"Here," Puck said, his voice low.

A second later, an ice pack wrapped in a soft cloth was being laid across my head.

"Drink this," Locke ordered gently, placing a straw between my lips.

I sucked down the concoction, the same one Puck had given me the first day we met. My eyes fluttered open. "You're the one who gets migraines."

Locke nodded. "When I stare at my monitor for too long."

"You mean when you don't break to eat or sleep," Puck chided.

My lips twitched. It was sweet how Puck clearly cared for Locke and wanted to caretake him. I sank deeper into the pillows. "That's nice," I mumbled, the haze of the migraine starting to pull me under.

"What is?" Puck asked.

"That you have each other." I let out a breath as my words started to slur. "I miss having people. A pack. I miss when someone used to care."

And then sleep swallowed me.

CHAPTER TWENTY-EIGHT

Wren

I WOKE IN THE CLOUD BED AGAIN. I FELT EVEN GROGGIER THAN before, but empath migraines did that to me.

Peering into the dim light, I swept my gaze across the space and breathed deeply. I didn't detect any of those now-familiar scents strongly enough to suggest they were in the room with me. Instead, I smelled…*bacon*? My stomach rumbled in response.

I swung up to sit, waiting to see if I got dizzy. Thankfully, there was none of that. I took in the hints of sunlight streaming in from the cracks in the curtains and wondered if I'd slept the entire day away.

Crossing to one of the windows, I flung the panel back, nearly blinding myself in the process. *Definitely morning.* I wanted to curse but felt so damn rested. It was the best sleep I'd gotten in years. Maybe since my mom had made me feel safe, even if that safety was a lie.

I turned back to the room, noticing a stack of clothes on the couch. I walked over to it and plucked up the note on top.

Thought you might want something fresh to change into. I had to guess at the sizes. There are toiletries and fresh towels in the bathroom. Hope you're feeling better. -L

A shifting sensation rose in my chest as if my organs were moving and rearranging themselves. I ignored it and headed for the bathroom, clothes tucked under my arm. Flipping on the light, I gaped. It, too, was a modern showpiece. There was a massive steam shower in one corner, and a huge circular tub in another made entirely of windows—ones I could tell were one-way glass. There was a vanity and double sinks, and the entire place was decked out in white marble with antique gold fixtures.

I eyed the tub with envy but wasn't about to take the time to soak when I didn't know what awaited me outside. So, I opted for the shower instead. Turning on the water, I stripped out of my workout clothes, grimacing at the fact that I'd been in them for days at this point. I piled them on top of a hamper and stepped under the spray, letting out a moan.

If anyone had heard me, I would've been embarrassed. But right now, I didn't give a damn. It had one of those rain showerheads that sent a steady stream cascading over me. My wolf snarled, wanting to play in the water, but also wanting to play with the wolves in her vicinity.

"Not today, girl." The truth was, I wasn't sure I could trust her to let me shift back, given how unstable she'd been lately.

I took my time washing my hair, shaving, and scrubbing every inch of my body. It was the best sort of luxury. One I couldn't remember ever having. My mom had struggled to make ends meet, and I certainly hadn't been afforded any luxuries while living with Bastian. While on the run, I was lucky if I managed clean and safe.

Tipping my head back, I let the water run over my skin,

soaking in the warmth. But I knew I was procrastinating, putting off the inevitable. Finally, I forced myself to switch off the water and step out of the shower. I grabbed a towel off the rack and realized it was heated.

"Wolves with too much money on their hands," I muttered. But as I wrapped the fluffiest towel imaginable around me, I realized I didn't mind their over-the-top tastes.

I made quick work of brushing my teeth and towel-drying my hair, then turned to the stack of clothes on the vanity. There were jeans that looked like they'd fit just about perfectly, a bra and underwear in delicate pale-pink lace, and a flannel shirt and tank that were both incredibly soft.

They all looked like things I would pick out for myself, except the brands were a hell of a lot more expensive than what I'd buy. I winced, doing some mental math on how I could repay Locke. As I did, I quickly dressed and headed for the door.

I paused before it, taking in the cowboy boots with cozy socks draped over them. They were a deep brown but had teal detailing up the sides. As I bent to stroke them, I felt how nice the leather was.

A burn lit in my throat as I pulled on the socks and then slid the boots on. They fit perfectly. Locke must've checked the size of my sneakers.

It was too much—all of it—but I'd find some way to repay the kindness.

Taking a deep breath, I twisted the doorknob and stepped out into the hallway. The scents of bacon and eggs grew stronger, as did the sound of voices. I followed both, noting that I was on the ground floor.

I passed what looked like an office and a library, then spotted a dining room surrounded by a wall of windows. As I stepped inside, all talking ceased.

Only four of the guys were present, and I let out a sigh of

relief that Ender was the missing one. At least I wouldn't have to brace for an attack on that front.

"No morning escape attempts?" Puck asked, a glass of orange juice halfway to his mouth.

I sent a smirk his way. "Like you wouldn't have caught me."

Locke winced. "I might've activated the sensors on the doors and windows on this floor."

Puck chuckled. "But I do love a chase." His eyes heated as if that chase would end in something more than capture.

My wolf let out a low growl, but it wasn't one of menace. It was full of want. Need.

"How are you feeling?" Kingston asked, his gaze roaming over my face.

"Good," I answered honestly. "Back to 100 percent."

That had the alpha looking slightly skeptical, but Locke cut in before he could say anything else. "Do the clothes fit all right?"

I turned my focus to him, even though Locke wouldn't meet my gaze. "They're perfect. Thank you. But they're also too much. I'll pay you back. It might take a little time, but—"

"You will not." The deep voice cut in from the opposite side of the table, and my gaze found Brix's blue-green eyes.

I lifted a brow. "Bossy, much?"

Kingston chuckled. "Not usually."

That had surprise flickering through me.

"Sit," Puck said, pulling out a chair. "I bet you're starving, and I made breakfast."

I lowered myself to the chair as I took in the spread in front of us. "You mean you made a feast?" I asked, gaping at it all.

"Puck does nothing in half measures," Kingston said, a smile in his voice.

"What would the point of that be?" Puck grumbled. "Okay, we've got scrambled eggs with sharp cheddar, biscuits, bacon, sausage, cheddar grits, and a fruit salad."

My stomach rumbled in appreciation.

Puck only grinned wider. "What can I start you with?"

"I'll take—" My words were cut off as a ball of fur leapt into my lap and instantly put its adorable kitten paws on my chest. "Well, who in the world are you?"

"That's Princess. She's Ender's cat," Locke said.

My brain short-circuited. "I'm sorry. What did you say?"

CHAPTER TWENTY-NINE

Wren

I WASN'T SURE WHAT SHOCKED ME MORE: THAT A TINY KITTEN had made her home with a bunch of wolves, that it was Ender who had brought her here, or that her name was Princess.

It was the Princess thing. Definitely that.

She began kneading my chest and let out a happy purr. I couldn't help but give her a little scratch behind the ears. The purring only intensified.

"She's so cute," I cooed. But as I studied her, I realized she wasn't a kitten after all. Her features were almost uneven, her legs and body shorter than a normal cat's, but her facial features were that of a full-grown kitty. "Is she some special breed?"

Locke shook his head, a smile playing at his lips. "No, she has dwarfism. Someone abandoned her at the local shelter."

"Who would abandon you?" I singsonged, letting my fingers sift through her fluffy gray fur. "You're perfect."

"When the shelter has cats with more complex health needs,

they usually call Ender," Kingston explained. "Sometimes, he fosters them until he can find a permanent placement for them, but with Princess, he kept her."

"That cat runs his life," Puck muttered. "He video calls her when we're on missions."

I blinked down at the adorable creature making herself at home in my lap. "Are you telling me that the most cantankerous of all of you, the assassin, is also. . . a cat daddy?"

Locke started choking on the sip of juice he'd just taken, and Brix thumped him on the back. Puck burst out laughing. "I'm only calling him that from now on."

"Be prepared to get an arrow somewhere painful," Brix warned.

"Worth it," Puck said, popping a piece of bacon into his mouth before taking my plate and starting to fill it.

"I'm still trying to process that the dark lord has a heart," I mumbled as Puck set a heaping plate in front of me.

A deep chuckle sounded, and everyone froze, turning slowly toward Brix. Puck's jaw dropped. "Did you just *laugh*?"

Brix snapped his mouth shut and glared at Puck. "I laugh."

"Once in a blue moon," Locke muttered.

"They're not wrong," Kingston said, breaking off a bite of biscuit.

I took my free hand and picked up my fork, spooning some grits onto it. As I took the bite, I couldn't help but close my eyes as a soft moan left my lips. It was the best thing I'd tasted in my life. I'd thought the sound had been quiet enough for only Princess to hear, but when I opened my eyes, I found four sets on me.

I swallowed quickly, my cheeks heating. "Sorry. It's really good."

"Birdie, you keep making those sounds, and I'll make it my life's purpose to be your personal chef," Puck growled.

I broke off a piece of my biscuit and threw it at him. But he simply caught it in his mouth.

"I could do this all day," he murmured.

"Don't make Wren uncomfortable," King chastised.

Puck sent him a look of mock affront. "I would never do any such thing. Birdie, do I make you uncomfortable?"

"Only when you say Guinness is a good beer," I shot back.

He glared at me. "Guinness from the tap and in the UK, my love. Not the drivel here."

Something about the words *my love* had my internal temperature ratcheting up several degrees. It was stupid. I knew Puck was just teasing, but I couldn't deny how every part of me wanted those words. Which made zero sense because I barely knew him. I barely knew any of them. Yet I yearned for them all.

"Wren, you okay?" Locke asked tentatively from across the table.

I shook myself out of my stupor, spooning another bite of grits with one hand while petting Princess with the other. "I'm good, just thinking about the fact that I missed work yesterday." I glanced at Puck. "Did you let Dina know I'd be out?"

He nodded. "Told her you had a bad migraine."

The familiar explanation made an ache take root in my chest, memories rising of all the times my mother had made that excuse for me as a child. "Thanks. Does anyone know what time it is?"

"Eleven," Locke answered. "Why?"

I popped a piece of bacon into my mouth and chewed quickly. "My shift starts at noon."

"No, it doesn't," Kingston said. His tone wasn't loud, but it was final, the alpha bleeding into his voice. If he really wanted to, he could force my submission. It wouldn't even be difficult because my empath status meant I didn't even have a tenth of the dominance he did.

Still, my eyes met his in challenge. "Excuse me?"

Kington's jaw tightened, a muscle fluttering there. "You're still recovering, and it's not safe. Not when so many dark mages got away."

I didn't look away or show even a flicker of weakness. "You

know as well as I do that wolves recover from this sort of thing in a matter of hours. A day, at most. It's been almost two. I'm fine. And I doubt the dark mages will attack in the middle of the day. They don't want to be outed any more than we do."

Tension bled into Kingston's neck, making a vein there pulse. "That doesn't mean they couldn't use humans to take you."

He had a point, but I wasn't about to stay cooped up in their fortress for the rest of time. "I can take care of myself. You've seen that."

"What I *saw* was you getting a blade to the gut," King growled.

Annoyance flickered, but I knew he was pulling the move out of care. "I won't be alone. Puck'll be working, too."

"I can take one of the booths," Locke offered.

I sent him a grateful look. "See, plenty of backup. I'll only be alone when I pee."

Puck chuckled. "We could use the buddy system for the bathroom—"

"Puck," I warned.

He held up both hands. "All right, all right."

King looked at Brix in silent question. It was then that I realized Brix must be Kingston's beta, and he was asking for his opinion. It was so different from how my father ruled. His opinion was the only one that mattered.

Brix turned that blue-green gaze my way. It roamed my face and felt almost physical, like a gentle breeze across my skin. My wolf threw herself against the walls of her metaphysical cage, wanting out. Wanting to get to him. I bit down on the inside of my cheek to keep her in check.

"A deal," Brix rasped. "She goes to work and the gym but doesn't fight us on staying here."

My jaw dropped. "You know I'm not a prisoner, right?"

His lips twitched. "Little Warrior, prisoners don't get a guest room."

I let out a huff of air.

"You have one of us with you wherever you go," Kingston added to the bargain.

My back teeth ground together. "Fine."

He grinned. "I knew you could be reasonable."

I did the only thing I could. I stuck my tongue out at him.

King barked out a laugh. "Such spirit."

Puck leaned over and squeezed my thigh. "Will it really be so bad being stuck with me?"

The contact had heat spiking in my blood, and I sucked in an audible breath. My wolf snarled, chomping at her tightly held reins. *Fucking hell.* It took everything in me not to shift.

Something had changed while I was unconscious. Maybe it was the injury or being so vulnerable around these wolves, but *my* wolf was losing it. If she went feral, there was only one thing this pack would do.

Put her down.

CHAPTER THIRTY

Kingston

I TRIED TO FOCUS ON LOCKE'S FORM AS HE HIT THE MITTS I held up for him. I knew he wanted critique to improve. I should've been jumping on that. Getting Locke to train was usually like pulling teeth. But the attack a few nights ago had spooked him, though I knew the true motivation was Wren.

It was the same reason I was distracted today. Three days had passed since she'd gone back to work, and it felt like one of my vital organs was walking around outside my body. The feeling was beyond brutal. And there wasn't a damn thing I could do about it other than text Puck dozens of times each day.

Even Brix was making it a habit to eat lunch and dinner at Arcane every day, and that bastard hated being around people. The only one keeping their distance was Ender. He'd disappeared for two days and come back even surlier than before. His rudeness toward Wren had only continued.

Wren took it in stride, giving as good as she got. But something was off with her. At first, I'd thought it was just nerves at living with us. Now, I was fairly certain it was something more. I could sense her wolf's edginess. When I suggested a pack run—something that should ease her wolf—she quickly shut me down. Something was off there, and I *would* find out what.

Locke's gloved fist slammed into my mitt, bringing me back to the present. He eyed me carefully before quickly dropping his gaze. "You okay?"

"Sorry," I muttered, dropping the mitts for a moment. "I'm distracted."

"Wren?" he asked.

I nodded. "Apparently, she's all I can think about. Not good when my head needs to be on the mages. And the bikers, and Red River, and—"

"King," Locke cut me off. "We're a team. We handle it together. It's not all on you."

But it sometimes felt like it was. I was the leader of this band of misfits, and if anything happened to a single one of them, I'd never forgive myself. "I keep worrying about her," I admitted.

One corner of Locke's mouth kicked up as he pulled off his gloves and reached for his glasses. "Me, too. But she's starting to snap at any of us who gets too close. I don't think she's used to being around so many shifters."

She was used to going it alone, but it was more. My wolf was hounding me to push Wren, get her to tell me what was wrong, and reveal the secrets she guarded so tightly. Something told me there was an endless stream.

I studied Locke for a moment. "You feel a pull toward her."

It wasn't a question, exactly. It was more of a prodding. I could sense that each of us felt a pull. Even Ender, who was being a dick about it all.

Locke's cheeks reddened. "I like her. But you know I'm not good at that sort of thing."

Locke's negative talk about himself had me bristling. "I'm

pretty sure she likes you best out of all of us. I think she's even said as much."

His head dipped. "As a friend. Not as anything more."

"A spark can light in an infinite number of ways. No two bonds are alike," I reminded him.

Locke's eyes flared, flashing silver for a moment. "Do you think she could be a potential mate?"

Shifters had existed for as long as humankind had, but we'd always had fewer females. We were in a better state than the dragons, whose females had gotten so rare they'd almost gone extinct, but our species still had to accommodate. It had become commonplace for a female to have multiple mates. She could even have multiple *true* mates.

"I know she isn't my true mate," I admitted, my wolf snarling at that. He already considered her ours. "I didn't feel the mating bond when I touched her or see any glimpses of our future."

"Me neither," Locke admitted. "But I care for her more than I should. More than makes sense for knowing her for less than two weeks."

I mulled that one over, trying to make sense of it all. "I've felt a possible mating bond twice before, and those weren't this...intense. Maybe the bond would be stronger with her. It still feels like a betrayal not to wait to see if our true mate finds us."

It had happened before. Wolves bonding with a potential, only to have their true mate waltz in years later. The effects could be devastating.

"I don't know, King. She just...it feels like she fits. Like it was all meant to be. Maybe the fates are bringing her to us because we don't have a true mate. Either way, she feels like ours. Like we're hers."

Locke was right. Many packs didn't have true mates at all. But no matter what, I knew I wouldn't be able to let Wren go.

As if I'd summoned her by thoughts alone, the door to the gym opened, and she walked in, a storm brewing in her eyes. I waited for

Puck or Brix to trail in after her, but no one came. Anger surged, a fury that stole all the air from my lungs. "Tell me you didn't walk over here alone."

Wren sent me a scathing look. "It's all of two blocks. I think I'm okay without the constant guard."

Her words only stoked my rage. "It's after ten. Pitch-black. The dark mages could've been lying in wait."

Wren tossed her duffel onto the floor and waved her fingers. Blue sparks of magic rooted in the water element danced across them. "I'd sense their use of magic, remember?"

"Would you sense a bullet headed straight for your chest?" I snarled. My wolf let out a vicious growl at the thought—at Wren being unprotected.

"Doubt having Puck walking next to me would make any difference for that," she snapped.

"Two sets of eyes are better than one," I shot back.

"Whatever," Wren muttered, grabbing hand wraps from her bag.

My wolf pushed at my skin, letting out a keening sound. That had me snapping to attention. He sensed something off in Wren. Something wrong. I crossed the room and got into her space. "What's wrong?"

She glared up at me. "Back up, alpha boy."

A low growl left my throat. "I'm not a *boy,* and you damn well know it."

"I said I need some space," Wren gritted out, her back teeth gnashing together.

"King," Locke said softly. "Don't push her."

My head cocked to one side as I tried to figure out what the hell was wrong. Wren's chest rose and fell in ragged pants as if her breathing was labored. Her face was flushed and sweat dotted her brow.

"Are you sick?" I asked, moving to place a hand on her forehead. Our kind rarely got sick, but anything was possible.

The moment my hand grazed Wren's forehead, she doubled over, letting out a sound of pure agony. Her skin was burning up like she'd been set aflame. "I need to spar," she gritted out. "It's the only thing that will help."

"Help what?" I demanded.

Her gaze flew up to mine. "Going feral."

Locke and I froze. Had she just said what I thought she had? A million things swirled in my mind as I put the pieces together. Why she hadn't shifted around us, the fact that she was so on edge lately. Wren was scared she would lose control of her wolf.

"Wren," I began, keeping my voice as calm and steady as I could. "When's the last time you ran with a pack? The last time you had touch of any kind?"

Wolves were pack animals. We needed contact with our kind. It kept us mentally healthy. If we went too long without it, our animals could turn on us.

Pain filled Wren's eyes—so much agony it could drown us all. "Years," she croaked.

Locke moved then. He didn't hesitate. Of course, he didn't. Because he'd been there. He *knew* what it was like to go it alone. How it could break you.

He moved to Wren and wrapped himself around her. She cried out in pain, but he whispered to her and her wolf, reassuring them both. "I know it hurts. But it's the only way."

Wren whimpered, shaking against him. "I can't hold her."

I knew she meant her wolf, and I let out a curse. "On the couch," I ordered.

Locke lifted her into his arms and carried her to the beat-up sofa against the wall, settling her in his lap. I knelt beside them, running a hand over Wren's face, feeling her scalding skin. "It's been too long. If you shift, you could lose control."

"I know," Wren rasped, her voice more smoke than words.

"You need contact, release." I did everything I could to keep my voice restrained and my wolf in check.

Her eyes flared, realization dawning. "You mean…"

"We're going to give you all the touch your body's been craving for years. We're going to make you come, and then you're going to let your wolf free."

CHAPTER THIRTY-ONE

Wren

Everything hurt. It felt like my need had turned on me and become a weapon. And as I stared into Kingston's pale-blue eyes, I couldn't say no. I knew if I did, I would lose everything. And the truth was, I didn't want to. I'd wanted them all from the moment I met them.

Maybe it was simply my wolf telling me she needed this—that *we* needed it. Physical connection was a natural urge for wolf shifters. Not something to be ashamed of. Yet something about giving in now made me feel weak.

"Say yes," King growled. But there were no alpha vibes in his voice, no force. Even though he easily could've used his dominance to force me into submission, he kept his wolf in check.

"Please," Locke whispered, his lips grazing my ear. "Let us take care of you."

It was Locke's tender words that broke me, shattered my last shreds of restraint. "Yes," I whispered.

"Turn her so she's facing me, brother," King ordered, a growl bleeding into the words.

My body shuddered as Locke shifted me, changing my position so my back was to his front, and I was settled between his legs.

Locke shifted uneasily. "I'm not good at—"

"She needs you," Kingston assured him. "Your touch. Ours together. Your wolf will guide you. I'll help."

A tremor racked me at the words. Locke moved on instinct, running his nose down my neck. "Easy, Little Warrior, we've got you."

He said the nickname in a different tone, a gentler one, making tears spring to my eyes.

"We've got you," Kingston echoed, his hands traveling up my legging-clad legs. The higher they went, the quicker my breaths came. King's knuckles grazed the apex of my thighs, and I let out a gasp. "That's it. We want to hear all the sounds you make. Want to drown in your moans and pretty little gasps. Want to make your body weep."

Wetness gathered between my thighs, my body crying out for exactly that.

King's fingers hooked into the waistband of my leggings. "Tell me yes."

"Yes." The word was more plea than anything else.

In one swift move, my pants were gone, the force of Kingston's action taking my sneakers with them. My ass hit the leather with a smack that had another surge of wetness pooling. I couldn't hold back my whimper. It was too much sensation.

"We're going to help, Little Warrior. Easy now," Kingston cooed, his voice skating over me like a pleasant shiver. "Locke, her shirt."

"May I?" Locke's fingers tangled in the hem, but he waited for my answer.

"Yes," I breathed, the single word a hoarse whisper.

Locke's movements were gentler than King's as he peeled back my long-sleeved shirt and workout tank until I was completely bare. It should've felt weird, them clothed and me naked, but I couldn't find it in me to care.

"Fuck," Kingston growled. "Knew you'd be stunning, but you're a work of art, Wren." His fingers trailed along the insides of my thighs, closer to where I wanted them. He inhaled deeply, letting out another growl. "And you smell even better."

I convulsed at his words as if they were invisible fingers stroking me.

"Locke," Kingston said, his voice dropping. "I want to know how her breasts feel, what those gorgeous nipples taste like."

Locke sucked in a breath, the sound—along with King's words—making my nipples pebble. Locke leaned in, one hand moving tentatively to palm my breast. His thumb circled my nipple as his lips ghosted across my chin. "Her skin feels like warm silk, and she smells like wildflowers. I feel her nipple tightening under my thumb."

Kingston's fingers trailed higher. "That's her body crying out for more, and we'll always give our girl what she needs, won't we?"

My body shuddered, writhing against them both. The words were too much. More than I could handle because, against all reason, I wanted that. To be theirs. For them to be mine.

"We'll always take care of you." Locke's voice deepened, and his second hand joined the first.

Kingston's fingers parted me, and I arched into him, letting out a whimper. "Please."

"Even more beautiful when she begs," he rasped.

Two fingers slid inside me. King groaned this time. "Fuck, brother, I wish you could feel how tight she's gripping me, how greedy she is for my fingers. You gonna take my cock the same way?"

My lips parted with a gasp as my back arched. Kingston's fingers pumped in and out of me, picking up speed as they twisted and curled. It was the arc that nearly did me in, the way those fingertips dragged down my walls.

"Soak my hand, Little Warrior. I want to drown in you," King demanded. And I wanted to give him exactly what he asked for.

King's gaze flicked to Locke. "Twist those pretty little nipples. Heighten her pleasure."

Locke's fingers instantly obeyed the alpha, and I couldn't hold in my cry.

"That's it," King praised. "It's time to let go." His head bent as he added a third finger, the pressure inside me mounting. His tongue circled my clit, making me bow off the couch.

Waves of sensation coursed through me, and it felt as if my whole body might shatter like a star exploding in the night sky. King's tongue teased the hood of that bundle of nerves, coaxing it free. I let out nonsensical sounds as my body writhed in time with both men. Their hands worked in perfect synchronicity as if there was a metaphysical connection there. And maybe there was.

King's lips closed around my clit. He sucked deeply as his fingers pressed against my G-spot. Locke's fingers pinched my nipples just as the first wave hit—a thundering crash of power, one I stood no chance against. I had no choice but to do exactly what King had ordered.

I let go.

I let wave after wave crash into me, fire and ice cascading through my veins over and over until I collapsed against Locke, soaking up his strength. My chest heaved as I slowly returned to myself, taking in the half-lit room around us.

Kingston's eyes were locked on me, and he slowly pulled his fingers from my body. And then he sucked them clean. Those light-blue eyes sparked silver. "Tastes even better than she smells."

My jaw went slack. "You didn't."

He flashed a grin that I could only describe as wolfish. "Gotta have something to tide me over."

"But you—don't you want—?"

Kingston shook his head and leaned forward to brush a gentle kiss across my lips. "This was for you. To give you what you needed. There'll be time for more later."

My throat burned. The male wolves I'd spent time with hadn't been like this. Especially the alpha. They took and took and took some more. They didn't care about how others felt, especially the females. "Thank you," I croaked.

"We'll always take care of you," Locke whispered in my ear, his fingers grazing the skin along my ribs.

It was almost too much. Pressure built behind my eyes, but I shoved it down.

Kingston pushed to his feet. "Locke's right. And right now, that means we're going for a run. Your wolf needs it. Ours, too."

CHAPTER THIRTY-TWO

Wren

I BOUNDED THROUGH THE WOODS, RELIEF FLOODING MY system at the feeling of having the wind in my fur and running so fast my leg muscles ached. At being…free. My wolf was no longer on edge; she was…smug.

She chuffed as if to say, "*This is all I wanted all along.*" She'd needed the contact, the release, being with others of her kind.

Kingston charged ahead, leaping over a log and showing off his incredible strength and force. His silver-gray fur gleamed under the moonlight, his light-blue eyes shining. He was a sight to behold, his wolf larger than any I'd ever seen. And just like his human half, he was bossy and protective in this form, too.

Locke let out a bark that almost sounded like a laugh as he ran beside me. It was as if he could read my thoughts about our overbearing leader. He was just as beautiful as King, his fur a reddish-brown that made his gray eyes look both haunting and captivating.

He didn't have Kingston's force, but he had remarkable agility, maneuvering through branches and brambles with alarming accuracy. Some part of me wondered if his wolf was running complex math equations that allowed him to do it.

I pushed myself harder, relishing the burn in my muscles. It had been too long since I'd run full-out like this. My dark-brown paws glimmered in the moonlight as I raced after Kingston.

He hit the creek full force, sending water cascading around him. I jumped in right after, Locke on my heels. We leapt and played, splashing one another and nipping playfully.

Finally, Kingston let out a low howl I knew meant it was time to return. The moon had shifted its position, telling me it was past midnight. My wolf whined a little in protest, but it wasn't the battle of being nearly feral; it was more a petulant sulk.

King let out a chuffing laugh and nipped my neck. The move was playful, but I yearned for it to be more. For him to sink his teeth into me in a claiming move, and for me to do the same to him.

As if he could read my thoughts, a low growl left his throat, and then he leapt from the creek, shaking out his fur on the shore. A moment later, his form vibrated, a blur of motion, until Kingston's human form stood there.

It was impossible not to stare. He was a sight to behold. All lean, defined muscle. Like a swimmer but broader. And I couldn't stop my gaze from dipping lower. Just for a second, I took in his thick length before I forced my gaze away.

King chuckled. "You can stare at me all you want. But we keep clothes in an old stump out here if you want to shift and change."

I let out an annoyed huff and jumped out of the water and onto the shore.

Kingston dropped a set of clothes in front of me. "You'll swim in them, but at least the sweats have a drawstring."

I felt a flicker of nerves before I brought on the shift, unsure if my wolf would battle me over it. But as I pulled on that side of my magic, she released the reins easily, letting out what resembled a purr. She was sated and at peace, something I wasn't sure we'd ever felt.

That knowledge settled deep into my bones as they cracked and shifted. There was only a hint of physical pain as I took on my human form again, then pulled on the sweats and tee. They smelled like Brix, which only intensified the ache in my chest. Tears burned behind my eyes.

"What's wrong?" Locke was instantly by my side, back in his human form and dressed in a similar outfit.

Looking at him and Kingston, I shook my head and forced the tears down. "I've never had this before. The feeling of being part of a pack. Not that I really am, I just mean—"

Kingston moved into my space, kissing the words right off my lips. "You'll always have a place with this pack if you want it." As he pulled back, he studied me. "You didn't grow up with a pack?"

I fought the urge to shift my weight from foot to foot, knowing that a show of discomfort would give too much away. Instead, I gave him the only truth I could—the smallest sliver. "It wasn't a pack like yours."

Kingston's eyes flashed silver, his wolf not liking that answer one bit. But I didn't give him a chance to press. "Come on, let's go. It's late."

"Puck's cranky," Locke muttered.

"You mean he's pouting," Kingston added, amusement lacing his words.

I looked between them. "You didn't—I mean, he doesn't know what, um, happened, does he?"

King chuckled, the deep, rich sound wrapping around me. "Afraid he could sense it. That sort of intense pleasure is hard to hide from pack mates."

Heat flooded my cheeks. I didn't actually know what a pack bond felt like. Even though I'd lived with my father's pack for years, I'd never been blooded in or linked to them because my father had said I was too weak to carry his name.

The memory had a shudder running through me, but I fought it off. "Who knew wolves were gossips?"

Locke choked on a laugh, but he moved in closer to me, not taking my hand but pressing his arm against mine, giving me his heat. "Don't worry about Puck. Deep down, he's happy about it."

But as we broke out of the woods, all I saw was Puck's scowling face. "You just had to have all the fun without me."

I couldn't help it; I burst out laughing. But the laughter died as I took in Ender's hard expression where he stood behind Puck, his mistrustful gaze locked on me. Brix stood next to him, mostly impassive but with a hint of curiosity in his gaze.

"Come on," King said, clapping Puck on the shoulder. "Let's get home. It's late."

Ender made a noise that sounded like a cross between a huff and a scoff. "Then maybe you shouldn't have been frolicking in the woods at two in the morning, leaving us to watch your asses."

Kingston's expression hardened instantly, his whole body taking on his alpha energy. He stalked toward Ender, getting up in his space. "I didn't once ask you to stick around to watch my back. You *wanted* to be here. Because as much as you want to lie to yourself and the rest of us, you feel drawn to Wren, too. Grow the hell up and deal with it."

Ender's amber eyes flashed gold, fury swirling there. "Just because I want to fuck her doesn't mean I trust her."

And with that, King's fist smashed into Ender's nose, breaking it for the second time this week.

CHAPTER THIRTY-THREE

Wren

I PULLED THE BATHROOM DOOR JUST SHY OF CLOSED, ONLY enough to let a hint of light peek through. Back at my apartment, I'd had night-lights, but I'd been embarrassed to pack and bring them here. I didn't want to answer the questions using them would raise. So, leaving one of the bathroom lights on was my only option.

Slipping into bed, I sighed at the feel of the soft sheets and fluffy mattress. While my wolf felt at peace, my human half was on edge. Ender's cruel words stoked fury among his pack mates. Now, they were all at odds.

It didn't matter how much of a prick Ender was. I didn't want him on the outside looking in—even if it was his fault. Because I knew how that felt, how lonely it could be. And something told me he was mistrustful for a reason. He'd been hurt before. I could feel it even with my emotional shields up.

A soft knock sounded on the door. The three raps had long

pauses between them, as if whoever was on the other side wasn't sure they wanted to see them through.

"Come in," I called.

The door swung open slowly, and Locke filled the space. He wore flannel pajama bottoms with some sort of video game design on them, a tee that stretched across the lean muscles of his chest, and those black-framed glasses. He looked adorable and gorgeous.

"Hi," I said, my voice dropping a fraction.

One corner of his mouth kicked up as he shut the door behind him. "Hi. I, um, I was wondering if I could sleep with you."

My eyes flared. We hadn't talked about what today had meant, not really. I got the sense that Kingston wanted more, but I wasn't sure about the rest of the guys. Well, other than Ender's crass offer.

I felt the most at ease around Locke, as if my soul sighed in his presence, so my words came quickly. "Of course." I pulled back the covers to welcome him in.

Locke quickly crossed to me, pulling his glasses off and setting them on the nightstand before sliding into bed. I rolled over to face him, my hands tucked under my chin. He hesitantly reached out and tucked a strand of hair behind my ear.

"It can take a while for the touch-hunger to leave when it's been that long," he murmured. "I don't want you to be uncomfortable."

My heart clenched as I put the pieces together. "You've experienced it."

It wasn't a question, but Locke answered anyway. "When I turned thirteen, and my parents realized I was a submissive wolf, they turned me out."

I sucked in a sharp breath, the inhale coated in invisible razor blades. "Locke."

"They're both dominant wolves. They didn't understand how I turned out the way I did and wanted nothing to do with me. I lived on the streets for about five years before King found me. He taught me that I have value beyond my dominance or submission. That I'm more than what my parents saw me as."

My hand found Locke's under the covers, and I threaded my fingers through his, squeezing gently. "You're so much more than that. We all are. Our value is not determined by physical strength. Our existence is so much more multifaceted than that."

I said the words for me as much as Locke because I wanted to believe them, even though I wasn't quite there yet. I could still hear Bastian's words echoing in my head. *"Weak,"* he spat. *"If I couldn't scent my blood running through your veins, I wouldn't believe you were mine. A waste of fur and air."*

My eyes burned as I remembered the feeling of his belt slicing open the skin of my back. The stinging, blinding pain.

"Wren," Locke whispered, his forehead dropping to mine.

"They don't see us," I croaked. "But we're still here."

"*I* see you, Wren. And everything I see is beautiful. Gentle *and* fierce. Strong *and* tender. You're everything all at once, and it's the most incredible thing I've ever witnessed."

That burn spread to my throat, making it hard to talk. "Locke."

"Sleep, Little Warrior. I'll hold you while you do."

And for the first time since my mom was killed, I went to sleep knowing someone was looking out for me.

I woke to birds chirping outside my window and the sun cascading through the glass. I blinked against the bright light, realizing I was alone. Disappointment flared, but as I stretched, I took in the feel of my body, my mind, my *spirit*.

I felt good. The best I'd felt...maybe ever.

Grinning at the ceiling, I let my arms flop wide. The movement sent a piece of paper on the pillow next to me fluttering. I snatched it up and read quickly.

Wren,

You were sleeping so peacefully I couldn't bear to wake you. Heading into town to do some work for Brix, but I'll be back after lunch. Maybe we can go for a run?

xx Locke

I kicked my feet beneath the covers, letting out a silent squeal. Giddy. I felt totally fucking giddy. Who knew snuggling with a wolf all night could turn me back into a middle-schooler?

Biting my bottom lip, I sat up and stashed the note in my nightstand drawer for safekeeping. I made quick work of getting ready and making the bed. This was my first day off since I started living with the guys, and I wasn't sure what to do with it. Maybe grab a snack and book and head down to the creek.

I opened my door and listened. I didn't hear anything, but it *was* after ten. I was sure they were all at work. I padded down the hallway, moving through the dining room and into the kitchen. I saw a platter of pastries and another note.

Birdie,

Had these delivered from the bakery in town. Wasn't sure what you liked, so I got options. So damn sorry I'm missing hearing the little moans you make as you eat. Reenact them for me later?

Puck

I grinned so widely that my cheeks started to hurt. I plucked what looked like a chocolate chip scone from the bunch and took a bite. The moan slipped free. At least Puck couldn't give me shit about it.

I finished my breakfast in a matter of minutes and then went in search of the library. It took a few tries to find it, but when I did, I gaped in awe at the rows and rows of books. I tried to figure out the categorization, but there didn't seem to be any.

A soft meow caught my attention, and I turned to the window seat to find Princess rising from a nap. She stretched, arched her spine, and let out another meow.

"I didn't even see you there." I crossed to the window seat to give her a few strokes. The moment I stopped, she jumped down and meowed louder.

A laugh bubbled out of me. "Are you mad I stopped petting you?"

She meowed again, the sound taking on a bossy tone, and then walked toward the library door. When I didn't move, she only meowed louder.

Amused, I headed over. "Want to tell me where we're going?"

She simply trotted down the hallway, and I followed. At the end, she slipped into an open door. I went after her, only to gape at the large room. One half was some sort of cat's dream jungle gym, and the other was an arsenal full of weapons of all kinds—bows most of all.

Princess leapt onto a cat tower, climbing from one plank to another before settling herself in a bed to look out the window. I crossed to her, scratching behind her ears. "You wanted to show me your house, didn't you? It's very impressive."

My hand dropped away as the weapons on the other side of the room beckoned me. I'd worked with blades and a bit with guns, but never with a bow and arrow. Seeing how Ender had wielded one in our fight with the dark mages made me curious.

I moved to the wall and realized quivers of arrows were lined up beneath them. I plucked one from its holder and pressed the point to my finger. Wincing, I instantly retreated, a speck of blood appearing on the tip.

I couldn't help but wonder if you could imbue arrows with

the sort of magic I could weave as a caster. Studying the arrow, I thought about the kind of spell that might work. I was so caught up that I didn't hear the footsteps. Or maybe he was so used to moving silently that he did it as a force of habit. Either way, the booming voice nearly made me jump out of my skin.

"What the hell do you think you're doing?"

CHAPTER THIRTY-FOUR

Ender

SHE WAS IN MY SPACE. INVADING IT. INFECTING IT WITH her scent. Wildflowers and rain. So strong now I wondered if I'd ever be able to get it out.

Wren's jaw went slack, her eyes widening as she gripped the arrow tighter. As if that would save her. "I, um, would you believe that Princess asked me in?"

I sent my cat a sidelong look. She licked her paw, looking pleased as punch with herself.

"Cats don't speak," I growled.

Wren arched a brow at that. "Yours certainly does. She made it very clear what she wanted."

My back teeth ground together because I knew damn well Wren was right. Princess had a way of expressing her every want and need.

A smile spread across Wren's face. "And what Princess wanted was to show me her house. You built her a cat castle. Or should we call it a pussy palace? That kind of has a ring to it, don't you think, Cat Daddy?"

I glared at the woman who'd done nothing but get under my skin for the past two weeks. Every contact I'd reached out to about her had come up empty. It was as if Wren didn't exist at all.

I repeatedly reminded myself that her ghost status meant she couldn't be trusted, but I feared it was too late. My brothers had all melted for her. Even Brix, the last person I would've thought would soften for anyone.

Shifting uncomfortably, I kept right on glaring at the bane of my existence. "She needs mental and physical stimulation. This structure gives her that."

Wren's smile only widened, and fuck if that didn't hit me somewhere in the vicinity of my chest. I'd seen her cast a quick grin at one of my brothers but not smile full-out like this. It was devastating. The kind of beauty that could bring a man to his knees. Maybe it was designed that way.

"You researched cat physical and mental health, didn't you?" she asked.

My glare only intensified because she was fucking right. "I don't see how that's any of your business."

Wren shrugged, keeping hold of the arrow she'd *stolen*. "I like your cat. She tells me you aren't the supreme ruler of all evil. At least, not *all* the time."

My wolf growled. He loved the female's fire, her feistiness. He had no patience for weakness or fear, and this wolf showed neither. "You don't know me," I said, my voice dropping low.

Wren simply stared back in challenge. "No, I don't. But you don't know *me* either."

Something about those words got my wheels turning, an idea springing to life. "You're right."

She blinked at me, shock evident in her expression. "I'm sorry. Did you just say I was right?"

"Don't get used to it," I clipped, striding toward the wall of bows. "You ever shoot one?" I asked, inclining my head toward the arrow in her hand.

"No, I—"

"Want to learn?" I grabbed two bows from the wall, my smallest for her, and my favorite custom piece for myself.

"Did aliens invade? Are you actually a pod person? Where's asshole Ender, and what did you do to him?"

I sent her a droll look. "No body snatching or anal probing today. I just realized you have a point. I don't know you at all. Maybe we should change that," I said, holding out the bow to her.

Maybe I would learn something that would give me answers to who this charlatan truly was.

"You want to focus on both the target and the arrow. Let yourself see both at once," I instructed.

We'd made our way to my targets at the back of the property. At least there was fresh air out here to dilute her scent. But I'd found it wasn't just Wren's aroma affecting me. It was everything about her.

The sound of her voice. The curiosity in her questions. The determination she had in every task that lay before her.

"Are you trying to make me go cross-eyed? I can't look at two things at once," Wren bit out.

I had to swallow my laughter. Definitely fiery. "You can. Open your vision. See everything around you. The trees, the targets, the forest floor, your bow, the tip of your arrow. Let it all in."

Wren inhaled, and I watched as she centered herself, trying to do exactly as I'd instructed.

"Now, release," I ordered.

Her fingers let go of the grip she had on both the bowstring and the arrow's nock. The projectile hurtled toward the target with enviable speed for a beginner and hit the target four rings out from the center.

I couldn't help the grin tugging at my lips. "See, hold it all at once and look what you get."

Wren let out a huff of frustration as she stalked toward the target to pull her arrow free. "I guess it's better than hitting dirt," she muttered.

I studied her as she stomped back to me. I didn't see her demeanor as an act, but I could be wrong. This could all be a woven façade to pull me in. Either way, I'd let her believe she'd ensnared me.

"You know, most people who pick up archery would be thrilled to hit the target on day one."

Wren's turquoise gaze flicked to me. "I guess I'm not most people."

I moved in closer, trying to ignore the scent of wildflowers teasing my nostrils. My wolf wanted to play with the female. He wanted to tease, toy with, and *bite*. That was inconvenient. And he would just have to deal with disappointment.

My gaze raked over Wren's face, studying it, ready to grasp any tiny reaction. "Why are you so hard on yourself?"

Defiance flickered in those captivating eyes. "I'm not naturally strong, not born dominant. It means I have to work ten times harder than anyone else to get that way."

My brows lifted in surprise. The first two statements weren't exactly a shock. As fiery as Wren was, I knew her wolf wasn't dominant. But that last revelation? *That* was interesting.

"And why do you need to be that way?" I asked, my voice smooth as silk, trying to lull her into an honest answer.

Wren lifted her chin. "So I don't get dead."

I chuckled, the sound breaking free without my permission. "Not getting dead is as good a goal as any."

Her lips twitched. "I am partial to breathing."

Gods, those lips. They were stained a deep shade of pink as if she'd been eating berries in the forest all day, and plump as if she'd been kissing for hours. Who knew? Maybe she and Locke had been doing just that in the early hours of the morning. He'd certainly looked pleased with himself when he exited her room.

My back molars ground together as jealousy flared. Fast on its heels came annoyance, then anger. "Again," I gritted out.

Wren lifted her bow and nocked the arrow as if she'd been doing it for months instead of minutes.

"Wait," I commanded. She stilled, and I stepped in closer. *Fuck.* I was drowning in wildflowers now. My fingers grazed her elbow. The skin was so soft. But I saw hints of those scars peeking out from under her tee.

I swallowed hard, trying to focus. "Lift your elbow. You form one long line. See?" I traced my finger from her elbow to her knuckles, keeping my touch featherlight.

Wren sucked in a breath, her head turning, and her gaze colliding with mine. Suddenly, a new scent teased the air, one that had my wolf growling with pleasure. Her need. I could smell it clear as day, and every part of me wanted more.

"Shoot the arrow, Little Warrior," I growled, the nickname so goddamn fitting.

Her head jerked back to the target, and she let the arrow fly. It hit center mass.

"I think that's enough for today." I stalked off without another word, too afraid I'd end up fucking Wren against a tree if I stayed. I'd likely get a blade in the back as a *thank you*. But some part of me wondered if it'd be worth it.

CHAPTER THIRTY-FIVE

Locke

MY FINGERS FLEW ACROSS THE KEYBOARD, BUT AMID THE sounds of typing, my ears were trained for any signs of movement. Any hint of *Wren*.

Brix had informed me that she'd gone target shooting with Ender. Who the hell thought it was a good idea to leave the two of them alone with weapons was beyond me. And I needed proof of life, stat.

The floorboards creaked in the hallway, and my fingers stilled as I listened. Footsteps grew closer, and I turned to see Kingston in the doorway. Surprise had my brows lifting. When we weren't on a mission, he usually spent his days at the gym, catching up on work. "You're home?"

One corner of his mouth kicked up. "So are you."

"Wren," we said at the same time.

"She's addicting," King muttered.

I couldn't argue that point. I'd held her all night, and it still wasn't enough. "She's target shooting with Ender," I informed him.

Kingston's entire body tightened. "She's what?" he barked.

I winced. "Apparently, she wanted to learn how to shoot a bow and arrow."

"Who thought it was a good idea for *Ender* to be her teacher?" King snarled.

I shrugged in answer, not wanting him to kill the messenger. A second later, his voice filled all our pack mates' heads. *"Ender, if anything happens to her, I will make sure you suffer."*

A huff of annoyance sounded in response. *"Relax. Your delicate little princess is just fine."*

"Says the cat daddy whose pussy rules his life," Puck shot back.

"What. Did. You. Just. Call. Me?" Ender snarled.

"Enough," Kingston demanded. *"Ender, you will make sure Wren returns to the house unharmed in all ways."*

"Whatever," he snapped and then threw up a mental shield to block us all from his mind. Kingston could've broken through, but it would've been an invasion.

"That went well," I muttered.

King sighed, scrubbing a hand over his stubbled jaw. "I don't know what's gotten into him lately. It's like he's at his worst."

"She affects him," I said quietly. "It stirs up all the betrayal and mistrust he's experienced over the years. And it doesn't help that we still don't have a plan for Red River. Not to mention, the MC and the mages are still circling."

A muscle in Kingston's cheek began to flutter. "Any movement lately?"

I shook my head. "As far as I can tell, it looks like the mages retreated and went home. The MC is trying to reform with whatever members are left in Tennessee."

"We'll have to watch that. You sent your tips to law enforcement there?"

I nodded.

"It'd be nice if they helped us out for once. Especially since this is the human variety of trash."

"I'll let you know when I hear back," I assured him.

King shifted his weight before speaking again. "And Red River?"

It was difficult for him to even say the words. The pack had stolen his sister from him. They also unjustly slayed both Brix's and Ender's families. There was so much evil in that one group of shifters.

We'd been trying to find a way to dismantle them for years. We couldn't take them on head-to-head; their sheer size alone meant they'd decimate us. But we'd found ways to disrupt them.

Sending anonymous tips to law enforcement about their drug and human trafficking operations. Even tipping off the IRS about unreported income. We were chipping away little by little, but I knew Ender and King were growing impatient.

"I zeroed in on their new drug-running routes from Mexico. I'll be sending a map to the Feds shortly. If they time the bust right, it should cripple them for a few months," I said, opening a map on my computer screen with the path outlined in red.

"Good," King gritted out. "Good."

But I knew it wasn't enough. It wouldn't bring his sister back or any of the countless others who had been lost to Red River's violence.

"Gonna go for a run," he clipped, but he was gone before I could say another word.

I sighed. He didn't need a run. He needed time with Wren. She made everything better.

As if I'd conjured her, she appeared in the open doorway. "Is Kingston okay? He seemed…off."

Damn.

I wished he would talk to her and open up. Maybe it would help. I knew what it felt like to lay my burdens down around Wren.

She hadn't judged me for what I'd been through; she'd made me feel accepted despite it all.

"He'll be okay," I told her.

Wren nodded but didn't look like she believed me. Her gaze moved around the space, taking it all in. The rest of the guys called it The Lair, and I'd give it to them. It definitely rocked the dark vibe—all the low lights with neon in places. Puck had even had a sign made for me that read *The Lair*, which I'd hung over my bank of computers.

There were two couches in the corner, a pillow on one for when I needed a nap between hacking sessions. There was a mini fridge within reach of my desk so I could grab my energy drink of choice whenever I needed one, and a couple of gaming chairs behind the massive desk.

"So, this is where you run the universe?" Wren asked.

My lips twitched. "I like to think so. Come in. Sit."

She slowly moved deeper into the room and took the seat next to mine. I instantly pulled her closer, wrapping my hands around her calves. The urge to touch her was too strong. All I could think about was how she hadn't had the touch she'd needed for so long. I wouldn't ever let that happen again.

Wren's expression softened, and she leaned closer, her lips just a breath away. Then she closed the distance. The kiss was featherlight, the barest touch, but I couldn't resist leaning in, deepening it.

Her tongue stroked mine, the taste of rain and mint exploding in my mouth as the scent of wildflowers swirled around us. She let out a little moan, and my hand slid into her hair. *Gods.* I wanted all of her. Wanted to drown in whatever this was.

A loud, accusing meow sounded, breaking us apart. Wren giggled, not a laugh or chuckle but a true giggle. The sound was so light and innocent it had pressure building in my chest.

"I'm sorry, Princess. Were your eyes assaulted by us kissing?" Wren cooed.

Princess let out another meow as if to say, *"Yes, they were."* And then she leapt onto Wren's lap. I'd never seen the cat take to anyone like this other than Ender.

Wren scratched behind her ears as Princess headbutted her chin. "I missed you, too."

"Hey, Locke, have you seen Prin—?" Ender's question cut off as he halted in the doorway to The Lair. A scowl instantly spread across his face. "Are you trying to steal my cat?"

Wren rolled her eyes. "I think your cat is just proving that she has good taste."

"I'm going to take her to the vet for a checkup because she's obviously dealing with some sort of psychosis. I'm sure medication will fix it," Ender shot back.

"Pretty sure the psychosis is yours, given you built a pussy palace next to a weapons arsenal, Cat Daddy."

I'd taken a sip of my energy drink but started choking at the words: *pussy palace*. Wren leaned over and thumped me on the back. "Now, look what you did."

Ender just glared at her. "Princess, come on. We're going."

The cat gave him a long look and then simply curled up in Wren's lap. She grinned at him. "Don't you know by now? You can't tell a cat what to do."

Ender let out a growl, turned on his heel, and stomped down the hall. Wren's laughter followed him out.

CHAPTER THIRTY-SIX

Wren

I MOVED THROUGH THE HALF-EMPTY TABLES TO DEPOSIT A plate in front of Ginger and another in front of Amos. My heart gave a little stutter-step as I took in the fact that they were holding hands. The older couple looked like they were back on one of their dates from high school.

A grin stretched across Ginger's face. "Ooooh, look at this burger, honey pot pie. I think it might be Gary's best yet."

"It's got nothing on my Reuben," Amos said, his lips twitching. Ginger eyed the sandwich on her husband's plate as if reconsidering her choice. Amos chuckled. "You wanna split?"

Ginger nodded, a beaming smile stretching across her face as she glanced up at me. "He knows I have a hard time choosing, so he always orders my second pick just in case."

A pang lit in my chest. It was such a small thing, but wanting to make sure his wife always had what she wanted most was a sacrifice, nonetheless. That pang shifted into longing, and I wondered if there was any way I'd ever have something as pure as what these two shared. "Pretty sweet. And I think it deserves a milkshake for you to share. On me."

Amos shook his head. "You don't have—"

"I want to. Now, what's your favorite flavor?"

"Strawberry," they said at the same time.

I couldn't help but laugh. "Coming right up."

As I headed back toward the pass-through window, I felt eyes on me. Locke's from his spot in the corner booth, and Puck's from behind the bar. They'd been on me every day since I'd returned to work. As if Locke and Puck didn't trust that I was up to the task. As if they didn't *know* I was fully healed.

The problem was that I liked the feeling of their gazes on me too much—the warmth that settled in different spots, the assurance that they were watching my back. I could get far too used to it, and that was a dangerous game.

"Head's still okay?" Dina asked as she thumbed through some receipts at the bar.

It took me a second to remember my cover story for missing work. "All good. I just get them once in a while." I figured it wouldn't be a bad idea to have that excuse in the arsenal, even if it reminded me of all the times my mom had used it before she'd been stolen from me.

Dina's head lifted, watching me as I put in the order for the strawberry milkshake. There was something assessing to her gaze. Not malicious in any way, but as if she was pulling back layers. "Bummer. I hear migraines are vicious."

"They're not a walk in the park." And that wasn't a lie. The ones I got from emotional overload were brutal.

"You know," Puck said as he sliced limes, a mischievous smile playing at his lips, "if you let me give you daily massages, I could work the tension right out."

Dina let out a snort. "The only massage you want to give Wren is slipping her the ol' salami."

I choked on a laugh. "Can't say I've ever heard it put that way before."

Puck looked affronted as he set down his knife. "There is no *slipping* when it comes to my dick, Dina. Only stretching because it barely fits."

My face flamed as mental images swept through me, but I shoved it all down. Instead, I turned and patted Puck on the shoulder. "Whatever you say, buddy."

"Stop calling me *buddy*," he growled, his voice low.

"Wren, that's harsh. Calling a man buddy?" Franco called as he shook rain off his jacket, Juan and Clyde following behind him.

Juan chuckled and waggled his brows at me. "Wren has never called *me* buddy."

Puck let out another low growl that only I could hear, making me fight a chuckle.

"It's good for his ego," I said.

"Damn right, girlie," Clyde said, sliding onto a stool opposite me.

I leaned over to press a kiss to his cheek. "Well, what can I get you troublemakers today?"

A mischievous smile stretched across Juan's face. "I don't think what I'm hoping for is on the menu."

Puck cut the lime with more force than necessary as he glared at Juan.

Clyde let out a hoot of amusement and smacked Juan on the back. "You might want to take that comedy show on the road, boy. You keep it here, and that knife's gonna be stickin' outta your eye before long."

"Listen to the old coot," Puck said, slicing again.

I rolled my eyes. "Don't let Puck intimidate you. I saw him snuggling with Ender's fluffball of a cat the other day."

Franco's brows rose comically. "Ender has a fluffball cat?"

"He does. And her name is Princess."

Puck leaned in, his breath teasing my ear. "He finds out you told these idiots that, there will be retaliation." Puck raised his voice so the guys could hear, as well. "No rule against having a cat *and* a penchant for cold-blooded murder."

"Jesus," Franco muttered.

Puck placed all the limes in an airtight container and stashed it in the mini fridge behind the bar. "I'm off." His gaze flicked to me as he moved into my space. "You gonna be okay, Birdie?"

That smoky whiskey scent swirled around me. The heady effect had my vision going a bit hazy. "I'm good." But my voice came out just a little higher than normal.

One corner of Puck's mouth kicked up. "Good. I'll see you at home."

And then, he was gone, taking his heat and scent with him.

"Okay, I'm just gonna be the one to ask it," Juan said, leaning forward. "What the hell is going on with all of you?"

Franco smacked him upside the head. "Nothing that's any of your damn business."

Juan shrugged. "Maybe not, but I got a curious mind."

"You mean a sex-obsessed mind," Clyde muttered.

"Amen to that," Dina echoed.

"A healthy appetite," Juan argued.

Franco just shook his head. "A need for a life of his own." Then he glanced up at me. "If you're happy, we're happy. And the way all five of them watch you whenever you're in the same room...it's like their hearts are walking around outside their bodies."

I froze on the spot. He was wrong. There was an attraction there, sure. Friendship in some cases. But nothing more. There couldn't be. Not while I was hiding everything about who I was.

CHAPTER THIRTY-SEVEN

Wren

"YOU KNOW HOW TO PICK LOCKS, AND YOU'RE *JUST* TELLING me?" I asked Locke as he drove through the sheets of rain, the night closing in around us.

Pink hit Locke's cheeks as he turned the windshield wipers to a higher speed. "I didn't know you were into that sort of thing."

"I want to know how to break into any building I want," I muttered. It would've come in handy all the times my father left me in chains. I shuddered at the reminder and shoved the memory down.

A small smile played on Locke's lips. "I can start teaching you tonight if you want."

It had been a week since that explosive day with King and Locke. King was affectionate but hadn't taken anything further than kisses and hugs. Locke spent every night in my bed, holding me tightly. In fact, he made it his mission to cuddle me at every opportunity.

The rest of the guys were keeping their distance. I'd expected that from Ender and Brix, but Puck was surprising. He still flirted and teased, but he never got close. I didn't want to look too hard at why that hurt.

Lightning flashed, illuminating the night sky. I shivered. "A lock-picking lesson sounds perfect." I paused. "Wait, is that why they call you Locke?"

His lips twitched, and he nodded. "It's how King found me. Needed someone to help him get into a safe. But he was the first person to see my worth beyond that."

My heart ached for him; the way his parents' abandonment made him feel like he wasn't worthy. *They* were the ones who weren't. I reached over and placed my hand on his thigh. "You're amazing."

Locke's gaze cut to me briefly before returning to the road, his throat working as he swallowed. "Thanks, Wren."

He pulled to a stop in front of the house, staring out at the rain. "You okay to make a run for it?"

I chuckled as I studied the torrential downpour. "A little water won't hurt me."

Locke shut off the SUV and palmed the keys. "Ready?"

"Ready."

We bolted from the vehicle, laughing like unhinged idiots as we ran for the house. By the time we reached the door, we were soaked to the skin, my hair plastered to my face. Locke struggled to get the key into the deadbolt but finally succeeded, and we hurried inside.

Our laughter continued as we spilled into the entryway, and Locke flipped the deadbolt behind us. I glanced down, wincing. "I'm getting water everywhere."

"It'll dry," Locke said. "Come on. Let's get warm."

As we walked deeper into the house, the lights went out. No, not just the lights, everything electronic. I froze, panic starting to seep into my veins. My breaths came faster, one tripping over the other.

Locke muttered a curse. "Lines must be down."

But I couldn't grab hold of his words. My lungs burned, and my fingers tingled as memories assaulted me. *The pit. So dark I couldn't see my hand in front of my face. Nothing but darkness and pain.*

My skin burned from the last whipping, my father's words still echoing in my ears. "I'll beat the weakness out of you." *I shivered as the rain came faster, pounding against the wounds on my back and stomach.*

A soft cry left my lips as I curled into a ball, the dirt turning to mud around me. I prayed for it to take me, to swallow me whole.

"Wren?" A voice pulled me from the memory, and hands tightened around my shoulders.

I moved on instinct, fighting against the hold. They wouldn't get me, not again. I lashed out with a punch to someone's torso. They let out a strangled *oomph* and then a curse.

"Wren," they said. "It's me."

I started to run. I didn't know where; I just needed out. Away. I wouldn't go back. Not to the pit. Never again.

"Jesus, what the hell is happening?" a new voice asked. Some flicker in the back of my brain recognized my British charmer, but the rest of me was too far gone.

Strong hands caught me. "Easy, Birdie."

I flailed, fighting against the newcomer, screaming.

"Bloody hell. Help me, Locke."

More hands. Holding me down. Keeping me in place.

I fought with all my strength until my muscles gave out, and my throat was raw. "I won't go back. You'll have to kill me first."

And then, I passed out.

CHAPTER THIRTY-EIGHT

Puck

WREN'S WORDS BURNED INTO ME, SCALDING IN A WAY I knew would leave scars forever. *"I won't go back. You'll have to kill me first."*

"Bloody fucking hell," I swore, catching her as she collapsed.

About half the lights flickered on, casting the house in an eerie glow. Our emergency generator had kicked on. It powered some lights, the heating and cooling system, the water heater, and a few other necessities like the refrigerator and security system.

I lifted Wren into my arms. She was so tiny, her form so slight that lifting her took no strength at all. I didn't want to admit how good it felt to have her body pressed against mine.

Gods, I'd missed her. Keeping a polite distance these past few days had about killed me. But the truth was, she scared the hell out of me. A woman had already destroyed my world. If something happened with Wren, I knew it would ruin me forever.

"What the hell happened?" I barked at Locke.

Wren didn't stir at my tone. Locke's face, already pale, went sheer white. "I-I don't know. I think she might've had a PTSD flashback or something. It was like she wasn't even here. She was somewhere else altogether."

Those words replayed in my mind. *"I won't go back. You'll have to kill me first."*

Where had she been, and what had happened to her?

Footsteps pounded down the hallway, and then Kingston appeared, looking furious. "What's going on?" He froze at seeing Wren in my arms, then instantly charged forward. "Was she hurt? What happened?"

I shook my head. "I don't know. She freaked out when the lights went out, started fighting me and Locke, and then just passed out."

Kingston stared down at her, brushing a strand of wet hair away from her face. "PTSD," he whispered.

As if to agree with him, Wren shuddered against me.

"We need to get her warm. A bath, maybe. Or a shower," I suggested.

"Bath," Kingston said instantly. "The one in her room."

I began moving in that direction. Locke ran ahead, and I could hear the water running before I even reached the threshold. The low light cast everything in a creepy sort of glow.

Wren stirred in my arms, curling into me. Her hands fisted in my tee. The action was so simple, but it dug invisible claws into my chest, pain flaring.

"It's ready," Locke said, cutting into my thoughts.

"I need to get in with her," I ground out.

"Here," Locke said. "Let me take her. There's no sense in you getting in with your clothes on."

I didn't give a damn about my clothes, but I didn't want the scratchy material of my jeans to cause Wren any discomfort. It took everything I had to let Locke hold Wren, even for a moment. It was only that we were true brothers—not ones bonded by blood that meant nothing, but ones of choice who had fought through hell together, building a trust that couldn't be broken—that let me do it.

I gently shifted Wren into Locke's arms. Then, as quickly as possible, I stripped down to my boxer briefs. "We need to get her out of her wet clothes."

"I can help," King said, his voice tight.

Together, we took off her shoes and unfastened her jeans as Locke held her upright. The soggy denim was difficult to pull free without causing Wren any discomfort, but we finally managed it, along with her blouse. I quickly climbed into the bath.

Locke lowered Wren into the water, and she let out a soft moan, her eyelids fluttering as she burrowed into me. My arms came around her on instinct, a protective urge surging to the surface. I'd do anything to keep her safe.

My wolf pushed at my skin, wanting out, wanting to slay whoever had hurt this female. A female I realized he considered *his*. That knowledge had fear digging deep, its claws seizing my heart. I shoved the sensation down and focused on Wren.

I brushed the wet hair out of her face as she shivered against me. Her eyelids fluttered again, and she looked up at me. But her eyes were unfocused.

"You're okay. I've got you," I promised. "You're safe."

She shuddered again. "Not safe. Dark isn't safe."

My arms tightened around her. "Why isn't the dark safe?" I pressed gently. We needed to know. Had to know who she was running from so we could protect her.

Panic flashed in Wren's eyes. "They leave me in the dark for weeks. There's no way out. They hurt me in the dark."

A snarl sounded from the doorway, and I turned to find Brix there. He looked like he was about to tear the whole damn room apart.

CHAPTER THIRTY-NINE

Brix

"THEY HURT ME IN THE DARK."

Wren's words pulsed in my ears over and over, each wave bringing a brutal, icy pain. Someone hurt her. Our Little Warrior. Our delicate little bird with her spirit of pure flame.

I needed to know who. What scum had dared to harm a hair on her head? I needed a name so I could hunt them. So I could cause them more pain than they ever thought possible. And then wipe them from the Earth.

There would be no more danger for Wren. No more threats. She would be safe.

"Jesus," Ender muttered. "Get your beast in check."

I heard the strain in his voice and knew he had heard Wren's words, too. They would mark him like they had me. Ender might like to pretend she didn't affect him, but I knew the truth. She affected us all.

I stalked toward the bathtub, fur rippling over my arms as I took her in. Wren lay curled in Puck's hold, wearing only a bra and underwear. Her skin had gone pale, making the scars littering her flesh stand out even more.

There were so many I couldn't count them all. Our Little Warrior had endured pain and torture. Endless amounts of it.

I knew what it was like to feel pain at the hands of another, agony and being left for dead. Death would've been a kindness.

But I'd crawled out of hell after the Red River pack's attack. After their enforcers left me bleeding out on my living room floor at the age of fourteen, only alive because Ender had found me.

As far as I could tell, Wren hadn't had anyone. She hadn't had a friend to help her battle back to the land of the living. She'd had to do it all on her own.

But she had.

Because that's how strong our Little Warrior was. She'd make it through this, too.

I had the bizarre urge to touch her then. To try to soothe her in her half-conscious state. It wasn't something I'd ever felt, that push for contact, for connection. I didn't do *any* of that. And it scared the hell out of me.

"What. Happened?" I demanded.

Locke shuffled slightly, and my gaze cut to him like the predator I was. He swallowed hard. "Everything was fine. We were driving home from her shift at Arcane, laughing and joking. She wants to learn how to pick locks."

Pain streaked across Locke's face. "We ran inside, and the rain soaked us. We were still laughing, but then the lights went out. She freaked. It was like she wasn't there anymore. She was somewhere else. She started fighting me and Puck."

Puck's hold on Wren tightened as if guided by instinct. "She said she couldn't go back. That we'd have to kill her first."

A growl left my throat, fur rippling as my canines pressed against my gums. *In time*, I told my wolf. We would hunt those who hurt her. We would make them *pay*.

"Brixton," Ender said, voice low and tight. "Control. You can't give your beast the reins right now."

We'd been friends practically since birth. We knew each other better than anyone knew either of us. So, he understood that if my wolf took over right now, there'd be no getting my human half back.

Losing my parents, my sister, and nearly losing my life had made my wolf unstable at best. And that was only amplified under threat.

"I don't know if I can," I gritted out. It was the truth. Something about Wren set me on edge—far more than anything else I'd ever encountered, even having one of my brothers injured in the field.

Ender's eyes flashed gold, and I saw shock and worry there. But it was Kingston who spoke. "I'm just going to say it. I'm sure it's what we've all been thinking. We've all been on edge lately. Felt a pull toward Wren that is beyond logic. What if she's our mate?"

The room went silent, and no one said a word as King let that bomb hang in the air. He was right, we *had* all been thinking it. But I knew the truth.

I couldn't be anyone's mate. I wasn't fit for it. And I sure as hell wouldn't curse Wren with my fucked-up self. Everyone would be better off if I stayed alone.

CHAPTER FORTY

Wren

My eyes felt gritty, like someone had poured sand into them as I slept. It was the kind of feeling you got after an especially hard sleep. I blinked against the light in the room.

The first thing I saw was Locke. He sat on the bed, propped against the pillows, looking down at me with concern. "How do you feel?"

My brows pulled together in confusion, but then it all came back to me, memories from the night before flashing in my mind: the lights going out, feeling like I was back in the pit, fighting Locke, and then Puck.

I quickly scanned the room. They were all here. Heat hit my cheeks as I remembered Puck holding me in the bathtub.

"I'm so sorry," I whispered.

"Birdie," Puck said, his voice firm. "You don't have to apologize for a damn thing."

I swallowed the burn in my throat, acid coating my esophagus. Shame. That's what fueled the pain.

The mattress dipped as Kingston sat. He squeezed my leg through the blankets. "We all have stories, Little Warrior. We all have demons."

I toyed with the edge of the sheet. "I'm not great with darkness. Between that and the storm… I'm sorry."

A growl sounded from the chair in the corner, and I saw Brix's eyes flash silver. "No. More. Apologies."

I snapped my mouth shut.

Kingston squeezed my leg again, reassurance in his touch. "His wolf is on edge. He's worried about you."

I pressed my lips together but nodded. Guilt swirled through me. I didn't want to cause any of them pain, even Ender, who might deserve a shot to the balls.

"Wren," Kingston began, and my gaze moved back to him. "Can you do me a favor and drop your scent shields for a moment?"

I stiffened. The guys might've scented my supernatural sides before, but I didn't make a habit of allowing it. I'd trained myself to keep the barriers up so none of my secrets could be discovered. The training was so ingrained in me that it had become second nature.

"Why?" I asked, suspicion lacing the word.

Locke shifted next to me, taking my hand in his and squeezing. "I did some research while you were out. There have been cases where true mating bonds were blocked because of certain shields. The wolves didn't realize they were true mates until the shield was dropped."

A buzz lit in my muscles, and shock coursed through me. I couldn't deny that I felt a pull toward all five men. One so strong it didn't make logical sense, given the short time we'd known one another. I'd considered the possibility that we might be potential mates, but *true* mates?

I shook my head. "There's no way."

"Then there's no harm in seeing," Kingston said calmly, his hand not leaving my leg.

I'd heard the stories. How with one skin-to-skin touch, you'd instantly know it was the mate the universe had destined you for. And in that moment, you would get a glimpse of what your future would hold.

My breaths came quicker as fear and anxiety swept through me. I was terrified of either outcome.

Locke leaned in, placing his forehead against mine. "It doesn't matter if we are or aren't," he said softly. "I want you. You have me, all of me."

A fresh burn lit behind my eyes. "Okay," I whispered.

I closed my eyes and focused on my shields. The scent and emotional shields were separate, but I had to be careful not to lower both, or it would overload my empathic gift. Grabbing hold of the metaphysical fabric of the scent shield, I let it fall.

The second it did, electricity zinged through my veins—fire and ice and deep knowing. My lips parted on a gasp as a moving picture flashed in my mind: Locke in a field of wildflowers, but he held the hands of a toddler. A little girl with dark-brown curls and light-blue eyes the same shade as Kingston's. He beamed down at her as she struggled to walk toward me, babbling out nonsensical chatter. My arms were outstretched, ready and waiting.

And then the image was simply gone.

Grief and pain swept through me as my eyes flew open. Because I wanted it back. Wanted to feel that pure joy again.

Locke looked at me, wonder in his gaze. "Mate," he whispered. And then his mouth was on mine. His tongue stroked in, his spicy-chocolate taste exploding in my mouth. I let out a soft moan as comfort and heat spread through me until a throat cleared.

I jerked back, realizing the rest of the guys were still there. That heat was back in my cheeks.

Kingston shifted forward, a soft smile on his lips. "So beautiful," he crooned, ghosting his knuckles across my cheek.

That foreign energy was back, zipping through me. All fire and ice and certainty. A new image filled my mind. I looked up into Kingston's eyes, now lined with wrinkles, taking in the gray threaded through his hair. He swayed us back and forth to a Christmas song as stockings lined the fireplace. "Merry Christmas, Little Warrior. Thank you for giving me everything I ever dreamed of."

Then that picture was gone, too. But tears sprang to my eyes. "How?" I whispered.

"Because you're mine, and I'm yours," Kingston said, leaning forward and brushing his lips across mine.

"It's bullshit. This isn't real," Ender snarled as he stalked toward the bed. He reached down and grabbed my wrist.

The energy was more ice than fire this time, the two sensations seeming to battle until they took me under into the images of the future. I gasped, the feelings grabbing hold before the pictures did. Ender's hand gripped my hair, just shy of pain as he pounded into me. The sun baked into our bare skin, and a creek babbled in the background, but all I could feel was him: his power, the force of how badly he wanted me. "Wife," he growled. "Look how beautifully you take me."

And then it was gone. Ender dropped my arm as if he'd been burned. "Sorcery," he growled. "This is some sort of caster spell, and I won't fall for it."

He stormed out of the room without another word, and all I could do was gape. Brix stood then, crossing to the bed. His expression was impossible to read, but those blue-green eyes swirled, both colors darkening. "I already know the truth," he rasped. "But don't worry. I won't saddle you with a mate like me."

And then he, too, disappeared, trailing after Ender. Pain lanced my chest, his words like acid poured into the wound. My gaze couldn't help but travel to Puck then, seeking out some sort of comfort.

But I didn't find my usual joking charmer there. Instead, I found a look of agony. Shadows rimmed Puck's green eyes as he stared at me from his spot near the wall. It was then that I realized he was as far away from me as he could get.

Puck's throat worked as he swallowed. "I'm sorry, Wren."

It was possibly the first time he'd used my formal name. And it felt like a dagger to the chest. But the next two words dealt the death blow.

"I can't." And then he was gone, too.

CHAPTER FORTY-ONE

Wren

THE HOUSE WAS QUIET. TOO QUIET. BUT THAT'S WHAT happened when a bomb of destined-mate bonds detonated.

I rubbed at my chest, the ache deepening with each moment of distance from Brix, Ender, and Puck. Ender, I'd expected. Even Brix made sense; connection wasn't exactly his thing. But Puck? That killed.

I listened for a moment and waited, but didn't hear anything. I knew Locke and Kingston were around somewhere. They'd tried to soften the blows of rejection, but they couldn't force the others to accept the bond, and I wouldn't want them to.

My hand curved around the doorknob and twisted. Stepping out into the late afternoon air, I let the scents of pine, moss, and the creek in the distance clear away the aromas that had been drowning me for the past twenty-four hours. It was a special kind of torture to scent all five of my mates and know that more than half didn't want anything to do with me.

My wolf let out a keening noise. I didn't know what I could do to soothe her. Tell her it would be okay? But I didn't believe that.

I made my way through the backyard and into the trees surrounding the gorgeous mountain mansion. Slipping between them helped. Being one with nature. And it would help my wolf if I let her free.

When I reached the creek, I stripped, folded my clothes neatly, and left them on a log. Then, I tugged at the change. It was slightly more painful this time, evidence of being at odds with my very nature. Only it wasn't me who had made that choice. I would've welcomed all my mates, even the one who was a complete ass most of the time. But I wouldn't force a damn thing on anyone.

My bones cracked, and fur rippled across my skin. Before long, I was something else entirely. I shook and stretched, ready to run. We didn't wait, my wolf and I. We pounced, paws eating up the forest floor.

I pushed harder, relishing the burn in my muscles and lungs. That hint of pain was a welcome reprieve from the agony in my chest. A distraction.

I ran until I didn't recognize anything about my surroundings. It still wasn't enough—not enough to distract me from the pain. But I forced myself to turn around and head back, only my scent trail guiding me.

As I reached the pack boundary, I felt the magic of the wards wash over me. I slowed a fraction to catch my breath. By the time I reached the spot where I'd stashed my clothes, I was moving at a walking pace.

I stood, staring at the clothes, wondering if I should even shift back. Maybe things would be simpler if I just stayed like this. My wolf curled her upper lip. It wouldn't be pretty if she came across one of those who had rejected her right now.

That was enough to force me into the shift. She was too on edge to remain in charge.

My bones cracked again, and my fur receded. The sun had sunk beneath the horizon, turning the day into my favorite twilight time of night.

I pulled on my clothes and shoes, then lowered myself to the log, breathing deeply. Maybe I was chicken not to return to the house just yet, but I still stayed where I was, regardless. I stared at the water, bubbling over the rocks without a care in the world. The sound was soothing, but it still didn't do a damn thing to ease the ache in my chest.

The wind shifted, and the scent of leather and spice teased my nose. *Brix.* I couldn't help the growl that left my throat at his intrusion.

Turning, I sought him out, bracing for a fight. But instead of a human Brix, I found a wolf. He was massive and as dark as a starless night. But his eyes were the same. That swirling blue-green.

The wolf moved slowly toward me, a predator stalking its prey. I didn't move an inch. The truth was, even if he tore out my jugular, I might consider that a mercy.

As if the wolf could read my mind, he let out a snarl. I simply bared my teeth in response. He didn't get to reject me and then show up acting all protective and possessive.

Brix prowled closer until he was only a foot away, and then the wolf began sniffing, scenting me.

"Oh, no," I gritted out. "You don't get to scent me after what you pulled."

The wolf let out a chuff as if to say, "*That wasn't me.*"

I sighed. "It wasn't, was it? It was your stupid human half."

The wolf sort of barked, and I couldn't help how the corners of my mouth tugged up. But it also got me thinking. "Can I try something?"

The wolf cocked his head to the side, wariness filling his blue-green gaze.

I knew Brix's human half couldn't handle physical touch, but what about his wolf? I lifted my hand as slowly as possible so the beast wouldn't see it as a threat. The wolf didn't move as I got closer.

My fingers grazed his fur, and a tingle lit, spreading through my hands. Fire and ice zinged through my veins, making me suck in a breath as an image hit me. It was as if I was seeing things from above. Brix's body was curled around mine, our limbs interwoven as we slept. It was the sort of position that spoke of sleeping together countless times. And then, the image was gone.

The wolf stared at me, wonder and confusion in his eyes. But my fingers stayed in his fur. The pull to heal him was almost too much to bear. My empath side roared to life, demanding to help.

The urge was natural, especially because this wolf was my mate. Wanting to help him in any way I could was woven into the very fabric of my soul. My fingers grazed his chest and the unbelievably soft fur.

I clamped down on the empathic pull because I knew if I tried to heal his pain, it would end me. But maybe I could take just a bit. I let little pieces of the darkness into me. It was like ink poured into water, swirling through me. But the ink was like acid, bringing with it a burning pain. I took it on anyway, pulling it into me and filtering it out with each exhale.

The wolf looked at me in wonder and then shoved into my touch, wanting more, wanting everything.

CHAPTER FORTY-TWO

Brix

Heaven and hell. That was Wren. Her touch was pure pleasure, but after going so long without pain-free contact, it almost hurt to endure the goodness of it. The light.

I pushed into the feel of her, her fingers in the fur of my chest. A warm, tingly sensation spread through me as if foreign energy was sweeping through the muscle and sinew. I was desperate for more of it—more of her.

A low growl left my throat as I rested my head on her shoulder. My canines ached to bite, to mark her as mine and cement the bond forever. Just that thought had me pulling back.

I needed to shift to give my human half control. My wolf couldn't be trusted.

The shift was harder this time, my wolf battling to keep control and stay with Wren. I didn't blame the bastard.

Muscles tore and reformed, the same with my bones. My fur

disappeared, replaced by skin covered in ink. Wren stared up at me, her gaze tracking over my body as pink hit her cheeks.

Fuck.

That blush was too damn cute. I wanted to trace it with my fingers and tongue to see where it led. I shook myself out of the lust-induced stupor and went in search of clothes. We kept sweats and tees stashed in various places around the property so we had them when we needed them. I found a set of sweatpants in a hollowed-out tree and quickly tugged them on.

Then I stalked back toward Wren. It was as if nothing could keep me away from her. The mating bond called to me. I'd known it before, but seeing that image of our future? Feeling the bond flare to life, even if it hadn't been cemented with a bite mark? Nothing could keep me from her now.

Even if I *should* stay away. Even if that would be the kindest thing for her. I couldn't. Wren's pull was too strong.

As I approached, she pushed to her feet, her gaze roaming over my bare chest and the ink there. It was only fair since I'd watched her from afar.

I'd trailed behind her as she ran earlier, staying far enough away that she wouldn't scent me but close enough that I could make sure she was safe. Her wolf was beautiful—unique, just like her. Rich, dark-brown fur with black around her eyes and a patch of white on her chest that almost looked like a heart.

Wren's turquoise gaze lifted to mine. "How do you have all these tattoos if you don't like to be touched?"

My throat worked as I swallowed. "I can handle painful touch: sparring, ink. All of that is fine."

Hurt flashed in Wren's eyes—pain, for me. She took a step closer. "Can I try something again?"

I bit the inside of my cheek so hard the metallic taste of blood filled my mouth, but I nodded.

Wren's hand lifted, and her fingers traced the edge of an inked blade that ran across my ribs. I braced for agony, but there was none. Just a buzz of foreign energy, a gentle wave passing through me, slightly lifting something inside me.

I stared at her in wonder. "How?" I croaked.

Her hand instantly fell away. "I don't know. The mating bond, maybe. Or my caster magic."

But the fact that she wouldn't meet my gaze told me there was something else. Something she was still hiding. Wren had layers upon layers of secrets, and I wanted to know them all. Yet I had no right to them. I hadn't given her a single damn reason to trust me.

I moved in closer, the heat of her body bleeding into me, her wildflower-and-rain scent strangling my throat. "My turn to try something."

Wren's eyes widened, and her lips parted. I didn't wait. My fingers slid into her silky, dark-brown hair, tightening on the strands so I could tug her head back. My mouth met hers with desperate need, my tongue sliding inside.

Her taste exploded in my mouth. She was rainstorms and mint—a tempest I wanted to drown in.

Wren pressed herself against me, her tiny form wrapping around my much larger one. A soft moan slid free, the vibration of it sweeping through me in a wave. I growled into her mouth, desperate for more of that, to know what she would sound like when she came.

Wren's legs wrapped around my waist, holding on for dear life. My dick hardened against her as she ground into me. My hands dug into that perfect ass.

Fuck. This woman would ruin me. But I'd happily go down in the rubble. For her.

Suddenly, Wren tore her mouth from mine, shock and panic filling her eyes.

"What is it?" I snarled, my wolf pushing at my skin at his mate's discomfort.

"Magic," she whispered. "I feel dark magic."

CHAPTER FORTY-THREE

Wren

BRIX SET ME DOWN IN A FLASH AS HE MOVED THROUGH the trees, reaching into a stump and pulling out two blades. He handed one to me and then scented the air. A curse slipped free. "They shouldn't have been able to make it through the wards."

"They're dark mages. The price they pay for their magic can get them through most magical barriers." I'd studied them as much as I could after coming up against one in New York. I'd almost lost my life because I hadn't been prepared. The only thing that had saved me was the early warning system I had built into me, thanks to my caster half.

Brix let out a low growl. "The guys are coming."

Oily, dark magic pressed against my skin. The weight of it told me we'd need all the help we could get. "There are a lot of them," I whispered.

Brix turned to me, fury making his eyes bleed silver. "Run."

Shock slid through me. "No."

"Wren, this isn't the time to argue. You will keep yourself safe, and that's an order."

I scoffed. "You might be my mate, but you're not my keeper. We'll keep each other safe. How about that?"

A snarl ripped from Brix's throat. "Stubborn."

"Damn straight."

The branches on the other side of the creek rippled in a breeze I knew wasn't natural. On instinct, I threw up a magical shield. Being next to the water would help since that element was my closest affinity.

The mages materialized then, all dark robes and shadowy features. One stepped forward, and I recognized him as the one I'd fought a few weeks ago—the one I'd injured.

A smile spread across his too-pale face. It was the kind of pallor that made me wonder if blood even ran in their veins. He gnashed his teeth as he took me in, his head cocking to one side. "She doesn't hide her scent anymore."

I didn't. Hadn't since the mate discovery. It had felt too painful to keep the shield up.

Brix stiffened at my side, his grip tightening on the blade he held.

"A caster," the mage cooed. "But also a shifter." His smile widened. "What a sacrifice she would make."

My stomach hollowed as true fear slid through me. Brix growled, dropped his blade, and instantly shifted into his wolf form. I understood why. He'd move quicker in that form and possibly be able to take out our opponents easier.

It wasn't the same equation for me. If I shifted, I wouldn't be able to hold the magical shield because I couldn't access my caster magic while in wolf form. I'd be able to watch Brix's back better if I stayed as I was.

The mage laughed, his head tipping back. "You think one single wolf will save you?"

I pulled on my magic, calling water from the creek and forming it into rope-like tendrils. "He'll have help."

Anger flashed in the mage's eyes, and he called out an order in a language I didn't recognize. The robed figures charged.

There weren't as many as the night in the parking lot, but there were only two of us now. It made me wonder where the others were. Worry gnawed at my stomach, but I didn't have a chance to wonder if the guys were under attack, too, because two mages flew at me.

They skated across the forest floor inhumanly, like ghosts hovering. I whipped my water magic, encircling their necks and pulling tight, cutting off their oxygen supply. They clawed at my water ropes, but it was no use.

A blow hit me from behind, and I sliced my blade across a third mage's torso. This one was female. She shrieked in pain, but her cry was cut short as the black wolf leapt into the air and grabbed her by the neck.

He whipped her to the side, the movement snapping her neck as she landed in the creek. Another of the mages screamed in rage, his magic blasting my shields. They wavered, crackling for a moment as the blow sent me staggering back, even if it was only against my shield.

Brix snarled, leapt across the creek, and ran straight for the mage. When he charged forward, the mage's eyes went wide. The mage lifted a blade to defend himself, but Brix simply clamped his teeth down on the mage's arm and snapped it in two.

The mage howled in pain until Brix tore out his throat.

"Caster wolf," the familiar mage whispered, his voice taking on the same oily quality as his magic.

I whirled, lifting my blade for protection.

The mage grinned at me, a disturbing look of glee in his eyes. "Such a unique blend. It'll be so fun to make that power mine."

Smoky magic swirled, its oily tentacles battering against the magical shields I'd thrown up. As I fought on the metaphysical plane, the mage darted forward, his blade raised.

"This doesn't have to hurt, caster wolf," he sneered. "I can make it quick."

I struggled to hold my magical shields in place. The weight of the dark magic pressed against them as I heard Brix taking on at least two other mages. My opponent sliced out, and I just barely dodged the blow.

My blade came down hard against the mage's sword, the clang of metal ringing out in the forest. We traded blows, matching each other almost evenly. But then more magic pressed down on my shields, and I felt the rest of the mages organizing in an effort to take the shields down altogether.

My focus slipped, only for a split second, but that fraction of a moment was too long. The mage's blade sliced across my stomach, and white-hot pain seared through me so much I started to crumple and fall to my knees. I knew if I fell now, here, there would only be one thing left for me. The end.

CHAPTER FORTY-FOUR

Brix

I felt her pain like it was a living, breathing thing. Like it was a part of me. Maybe it was the mating bond, or maybe it was simply the power of Wren. Whatever it was, I knew the instant she was wounded.

A red haze slipped over my vision, my wolf fully taking the reins as I let out a howl I knew could be heard for miles. That mage had hurt her. Spilled her blood. My *mate*.

Now, he would die for it.

I leapt across the creek, flying toward the robed figure. His dark eyes went wide, and he screamed for help. But they were no match for my rage.

One stepped into my path. I seized him by the shoulder, shaking him so hard his neck snapped in the blink of an eye. Mages might be magical beings, but they were humans at the heart of it. They needed their spinal columns just like everyone else.

A second lifted a sword to bring down on my neck. I dodged

his blow, leapt into the air, and sank my teeth into his carotid. I ripped his throat out, the taste of his blood coating my tongue.

The mage who had hurt my mate backed up in panic, calling for more aid as he raised his blade in defense. A coward, believing everyone else should die for his sins. But his sycophants were only too happy to do it.

Two more mages stepped between us. I curled my lip and bared my teeth, letting out a low growl.

One tried to throw a ball of black magic at me, but it turned to nothing but air, Wren's shield still in place. Panic lit in the female mage's eyes as she unsheathed her sword, but it was too late for her.

I charged at the male, teeth sinking into his side as I whipped him into her. His sword sliced at her skin, making her howl in pain the way Wren had. But it wasn't enough, not even the feel of the male's neck snapping was.

My beast craved every last ounce of their blood. He wanted to drown in it—until there was no longer a threat to his mate.

I dropped the male to the forest floor, the female writhing in pain next to him. I didn't wait. My paw punched through her chest, claws digging into her still-beating heart and ripping it from her body with a snarl.

The mage who had hurt my mate glanced around in panic, realizing no one was left to help. I prowled forward. I would take my time with this one. I would make him hurt for days. I was poised to attack, but there was an explosion of smoke, and the mage vanished in front of my eyes.

I growled in fury. I'd heard stories of dark mages with enough strength to do such a thing, but I'd never seen it with my own eyes. Rage flooded my system as I snapped at the remnants of smoke.

Shouts sounded, and I moved on instinct, placing myself between the voices and Wren. No one else would hurt her. No one would cause her pain.

Four figures burst through the trees, weapons raised. Some part of my brain recognized them as pack mates, but I still couldn't get myself to back down. The urge to protect Wren at any cost was too strong.

Kingston scanned our surroundings. "What the hell happened? Where are they?"

I shoved my wolf down as hard as I could, bringing on the change with more pain than usual. My bones cracked, and muscles rearranged as my fur receded and turned to skin.

All four of my pack mates stared at me, gaping. Puck scanned me from head to toe. "I'm pretty sure Brix is currently taking a bath in their blood."

I could feel it then, the sticky substance coating my skin. Memories of Wren's cries of pain filled my mind, and I struggled to keep from shifting again. "They. Hurt. Her," I snarled.

Kingston instantly moved then, trying to approach Wren. A snarl left my throat as I bared my teeth at my alpha.

"It's okay," Wren's soft voice said. "I'm okay."

Her hand gently landed on my back, and the feeling of it brought a sense of peace I'd never known. My eyes fell closed for the briefest moment as I soaked in the feel of her.

Then Puck's voice cut into my peace. "Holy fuck. Is she touching him?"

CHAPTER FORTY-FIVE

Wren

THE SHOCK IN PUCK'S WORDS HAD MY GAZE SNAPPING to him for a moment. His green eyes showed genuine disbelief, and his jaw had slackened at the vision in front of him. But I couldn't think about that right now. I needed to help Brix.

I moved, coming to stand in front of him, my hands going to his stubbled cheeks. "Look at me. I'm right here. I'm fine."

I could still feel the sting of the slice in my stomach. But it wasn't horribly deep, and I could already feel the tissue knitting back together. All Brix needed to hear right now was that I was all right.

"Wren, you need to back away," King said, his voice low. "Brix can be unstable when—"

Brix snarled, snapping his teeth at Kingston, even though he was in his human form.

Shit.

"All of you need to back up. Brix and I are fine, but we need some space," I ordered.

"Wren," Locke protested.

"Trust me," I begged.

Instinct guided me more than anything. I knew that Brix's animal side couldn't handle anyone getting too close right now. Not when he'd just felt the bond for the first time *and* had seen me get hurt. He'd do whatever it took to keep his mate safe—to keep *me* safe.

Surprisingly, it was Ender who spoke. "Back up," he commanded.

My gaze flicked to him in thanks, but he quickly averted his eyes. I tried not to let that sting. Instead, I focused on Brix. I dropped my hands from his face but wove our fingers together.

The first thing was getting the blood off him. It was only a reminder of what had happened. To get him calm and at peace, he needed to be clean.

"Come on," I whispered, tugging Brix toward the house. He went easily, sticking close as he scanned the surrounding woods. I knew he was looking for any signs of an impending attack, but none came.

We slipped inside the house, and I led Brix straight to my room and into the bathroom. I didn't let go of his hand as I started the water and waited for it to get warm. I met his gaze, holding it. "I'm going to let go for just a second to get undressed, okay? I'm not going anywhere."

Brix gnashed his teeth together but jerked his head in a nod.

I quickly stripped out of my clothes, the movement making the wound on my stomach sting and burn. I should've caught my wince, but I didn't.

Brix was up in my space in a flash. "You're hurt."

"I'm okay. Really. I promise. I just—"

"He. Cut. You," Brix snarled, struggling to keep his breathing even. Fur rippled over his arms, and I knew if I wasn't careful, I would have a fully shifted wolf in my bathroom.

"Breathe with me," I told him, lifting my hands to cup his face again.

Brix's fingers wrapped around one of my wrists, and he gently pulled my hand away, staring at it as if it were some sort of miracle. "How? You touch me, and it doesn't make me want to die."

My heart shattered for him. How long had it been since he'd simply been held? If I thought my wolf was on edge, I couldn't imagine how his felt. The only touch they'd been able to endure was that of pain.

Brix studied my palm as if it held all the answers in the world, and then his head dipped. He pressed his lips to the skin there. The mating bond sang, zipping through my nerve endings and waking ones I hadn't even known existed. I'd heard that touch felt different with your mate, that everything was *more* once you realized the bond—even if it hadn't been cemented.

I felt it now. That *more*.

"We need to get you clean," I croaked. I wanted to give Brix a little of what he was giving me. The knowledge that we were no longer alone in this world. We had each other, and we always would.

Brix moved then, tugging me into the shower, already filled with steam. He ducked under the spray, letting it run over him and wash the blood away. I knew I should avert my gaze but couldn't. The longer strands of dark-brown hair looked black now as he tipped his head back. That knife tattoo by his eye danced as the water hit his face.

I followed the water's path as it slid down his body, a form that was a finely tuned weapon. Big and broad but pure muscle. And those ridges and valleys were covered in ink, tattoos that told intricate stories of pain and triumph. My fingers itched to trail over every inch.

I reached for the bodywash, squirting some into my hand to create suds. I moved into Brix, my hands lifting to his chest. Those blue-green eyes locked with mine. The moment my palm connected with his pecs, the bond sang through me.

"You feel that," Brix growled low.

It sounded more like a command than a question, but I answered anyway. "I feel it. It's the bond."

Wonder filled Brix's eyes as he studied me. "You should've run when you had the chance, Little Warrior. Because now that I know what it's like to have your touch? You'll never be free."

CHAPTER FORTY-SIX

Wren

I sucked in a breath at the intensity blazing in Brix's eyes and the warning there, but my hands didn't drop from his chest as the water beat down on us.

"I'm the last thing you need, but it's too late for you now. Now that I know what you taste like, the feeling of those fingers humming along my skin…" Brix rasped.

My eyes flared, and I felt the defiance filling them. "You're exactly what I need."

And I knew that was true. Because the universe and fates wouldn't bond me to someone who didn't balance me in some way. The same way I would balance them. We could find a wholeness together that we'd never be able to find apart.

Brix's eyes flashed silver. "You don't know what you're playing with, Little Warrior."

My gaze didn't move from his. "I'm not scared of you."

Brix moved in a flash, his hands locking around my wrists and pinning them above my head. "You should be."

My back and arms pressed against the tile, the coolness of the surface at war with my overheated skin. "Do your worst."

Brix's mouth met mine in a hard kiss. It was all demand and dominance, but I gave as good as I got. Our tongues dueled for supremacy, and I didn't hold back my moan at the promise of all that was him.

The sound sent vibrations through us both, and Brix answered with a growl as he pressed his body to mine. His dick hardened against my belly, thick and long. The feel of it had wetness pooling between my thighs.

Brix tore his mouth from mine with a snarl. "I can smell you. Tell how much you want me, want this."

My breaths came in ragged pants. "I do."

One of Brix's hands left my wrists and trailed down my arm, dipping to my neck. His fingers collared my throat, tightening for only a moment. "Tell me again."

"I want you," I rasped. "I want this."

He released my neck, trailing lower, over my collarbone to my breast. He palmed it, his thumb circling my nipple. "So fucking perfect. Filling my hand, your pretty little nipple hardening at my touch, straining to get to me, wanting all my attention."

Brix's head dipped, and he pulled that bud into his mouth, sucking deeply. My back arched in response, a moan slipping free as more wetness gathered between my thighs. Brix's teeth grazed my nipple as he released it.

"The sounds you make," he ground out. "So perfect. Just like the rest of you."

"Brix," I breathed. "Please."

"You begging? Could bring me to my knees."

My breaths came quicker as his scent wrapped around me. All leather and spice.

He trailed his hand lower, his features hardening as he stopped just shy of the slash across my stomach. His other hand left my wrists, and he dropped to his knees. He gripped my hips, fingers digging in as his lips grazed the wound, featherlight. "This will never happen again. No one will ever touch you. Nobody will hurt you."

My fingers sank into his hair, the silky strands heavy with water. "It doesn't even hurt anymore."

It wasn't a lie. The flesh had knitted even quicker than it usually did. I'd heard about this, too. How being in your mate's—or mates'—vicinity could make you heal faster, but I'd never seen it happen before.

Brix's hand moved then, his knuckles grazing my slit.

My back bowed again. "Brix."

He slowly parted me. "Say it again."

"Brix."

Two fingers slid inside, and he cursed. "You feel like heaven. Wet. Tight. Mine."

My mouth fell open as I struggled for breath. "It's been a long time." The truth was, my experience was more than limited. And none of it all that good.

A low growl left Brix's throat. "Good." Those fingers drove deeper as he leaned in, inhaling. "Fucking heaven."

Brix's tongue flashed out, lashing against my clit. I couldn't hold back my cry. He circled that bundle of nerves, teasing and toying. My hips arched, seeking more pressure. Brix growled again, sending a wave of sensation crashing through me.

My walls fluttered around his fingers, and Brix tore his mouth away from me. "Not yet."

My fingertips dug into his shoulders as I tried to hold back my orgasm. Brix stared up at me, his eyes pure silver now. His fingers circled inside me. "Need you ready, Little Warrior. Ready to take me. All of me."

I sucked in a breath, my lips parting as I gave myself over to the delicious stretch. "Please," I begged.

"My little wolf is greedy, just how I like her." Brix's fingers were gone, and then he was on his feet again. He lifted one of my legs, balancing it on the bench in the shower as his gaze collided with mine. "Tell me I can have you."

"Yes," I breathed.

He didn't wait. He slid into me with a force that was anything but gentle. It was rough and more than a little animalistic—like the man himself. But it was everything I needed.

My hips thrust into him, meeting each movement. Brix's fingers slid into my hair as he took me, gripping tightly, just shy of the point of true pain. Between that and the girth of this man, my eyes began to water.

It was all too much—in the best way.

Brix cursed. "Taking me so beautifully. All of me. Like you were made for me."

"Because I was," I croaked. "Like you were made for me."

My words snapped something in Brix. He picked up his speed, his thrusts getting wilder as my walls began to flutter.

"Tell me I can mark you," Brix growled.

That only intensified the fluttering. It wouldn't be a bond mark, but it was still a claiming—one that would fade with time. But while I wore it, the mark would tell the supernatural world that I belonged to someone. I craved that. Just like I craved marking him right back.

"Yes." The word was just a whisper, but it was all Brix needed.

His canines lengthened and sank into the sensitive spot between my neck and shoulder. The moment his teeth met my skin, pleasure flooded me. My blood sang, and my nerve endings went haywire. I clamped down on Brix, and he let out a snarl I knew the rest of the house had to hear.

But I couldn't find it in me to care. Brix sucked on my claiming mark, wringing out more and more pleasure, heightening every thrust and wave. And as the last of my orgasm faded, I knew that everything had changed.

CHAPTER FORTY-SEVEN

Puck

I PACED THE LIVING ROOM, FIGHTING THE URGE TO RIP ONE of my brothers' heads off. My wolf had never been more on edge. He'd been riding me ever since I'd walked out on Wren.

We were usually of the same mind, especially when it came to women. He'd grown wary of females of any species after Alice, just like I had. We'd flirt and fuck but never get attached. We certainly had no interest in mating after the last go turned out so badly.

Until Wren.

I should've known from the beginning that the pull I felt to her was different. It felt like *more*. I should've run.

But I hadn't. And now, my wolf wanted to go to her. He wanted to bite her. Claim her permanently. It didn't matter that she was currently with my brother.

A light moan filled the air, and everyone in the room froze.

"Fuck," Kingston muttered, squeezing the back of his neck.

My dick went half-mast at the sound of Wren, at the knowledge of what my brother was likely doing to her right now.

"She touched him," I ground out, my voice tight.

Kingston's gaze cut to me. "She did."

"It shouldn't be a surprise," Locke cut in. "She's different."

"It's the mating bond," Ender said, strain wrapping around his vocal cords. "It changes things. Messes with all our minds."

Locke glared in the assassin's direction. "The fact that she's our true mate just means the bond is deeper. It's not a manipulation."

Ender scoffed. "That's what you think."

"Enough," Kingston said, exhaustion clear in his voice. "We have more important things to discuss. Like how the hell the dark mages got through our wards."

Ender scowled. "Need to have a word with Helena about that."

"They must've gotten some extra juice somehow," I muttered, not wanting to think about exactly how because it likely meant many innocent lives were lost to feed their dark magic.

Locke frowned at his tablet. "I think we need to go the tech route with this."

"That's always your solution," Ender groused.

"Because it works," Locke shot back.

Ender pinned him with a hard stare. "Unless they can knock out your system."

Locke stiffened. His system had only been defeated once before, and Ender's statement was fighting words. "I'm going to create two. So, if one gets taken down, there will be another, less visible one."

A smile spread across King's face. "Fake them out?"

Locke nodded. "We have our normal cameras in trees and then disguise others. Pine cones, rocks, in the branches themselves."

Ender's face screwed up. "Why not a fake deer or two, as well?"

Locke glared at him. "It's not like you're coming up with any solutions."

"We kill them," Ender stated with finality.

That was always his answer. Go on the warpath.

"And where exactly are you going to find them?" Kingston asked. "You saw that last one disappear into a cloud of smoke just like I did."

Ender's back teeth ground together. "I can track him. I just need time."

"You need a trace," Kingston pressed. "And there isn't one if he disappeared into another dimension."

Ender stalked to the window as if he could make the dark mage appear by force of will alone.

"We need to do some research. Find out how we can drain the power they get," Kingston went on.

But his words halted as a snarl pierced the air. No one braced for attack because the sound had a distinctly sexual tone.

"Jesus," I muttered, running a hand through my hair and tugging on the strands.

The ringing of a phone brought me back from the edge—an edge where I was tempted to charge up the stairs and join Wren and Brix. *Fuck.*

Ender pulled his cell from his pocket and glanced at the screen. "I need to take this." He stalked out the French doors, slamming them behind him. More like he needed some air. Just like the rest of us.

Kingston stared after him. "It's not good for him to deny who she is to him. Not good for his wolf either." He turned that stare on me. I read the judgment in it.

I fought the urge to squirm. Because I knew I'd fucked up. I just didn't know how to get past the wall that would live between Wren and me—between me and any mate.

Mate.

Fucking hell. I'd found my true mate. A gift so many never got. And I was wishing it all away.

But even as I thought that, I knew I couldn't wish Wren away.

Not how she gave me shit and could kick the asses of men four times her size. Not her kindness or ferocity.

"Trust doesn't come easy for me," I rasped.

Kingston moved closer, clapping me on the shoulder and squeezing hard. "I know. But it should be a comfort that it doesn't come easy for her either. Maybe you two can find it together."

Footsteps sounded, and we all turned toward the entryway. Wren and Brix appeared, freshly showered and dressed, but I could still scent the sex clinging to them. And I'd never seen Brix look… lighter. Happier.

Wren shifted from foot to foot as she scanned the room nervously. Brix pressed a kiss to the top of her head. "It's okay," he whispered to her.

Wren swallowed hard. "Everyone's okay?"

Kingston smiled gently at her. "We're all good."

"I'm not." The words were out of my mouth before I could stop them. Wren's gaze cut to me, and I saw worry in her eyes. But I was already moving. "Can we talk?"

CHAPTER FORTY-EIGHT

Wren

My heart hammered against my ribs as I stared at Puck. I couldn't read his expression, and there was none of his typical mirth or playfulness. Everything about him read: guarded.

I steeled myself and nodded. "Okay."

Puck didn't touch me, just gestured for me to follow him across the hall and into the kitchen. A heavier sensation settled into my stomach with each step I took, all sorts of scenarios taking root in my mind. The worst involved Puck rejecting me for good.

My wolf bared her teeth at that. Her solution was to simply bite him so he was ours forever. But it wasn't that simple, and I'd never take away someone's choice—their free will. Because it had been done to me too many times to count.

I crossed to the island, leaning against it in case I needed something solid to prop me up.

Puck cleared his throat. "Your stomach. Is it okay?"

For a second, I thought he meant the heaviness there, but then I remembered the wound. I lifted my tee to reveal my belly. The usual scarred flesh crisscrossed my stomach, but this injury was hardly deep at all. It would fade into nothing. Even now, it was little more than a red line.

Puck's blond brows pulled together in confusion. "That's too fast. How—?"

"The mating bond." My voice dropped. "I was, um, close to Brix, so it healed faster than normal."

Puck's lips twitched. "Close, huh? Is that what the kids are calling it these days?"

I choked on a laugh, but my cheeks heated.

"There's nothing to be embarrassed about, Birdie. It's natural that you want to be with him. With all of us."

My gaze lifted, taking him in. Memories of the past few weeks with Puck drifted through my mind. His kindness with my migraines, how he cooked for me, how he made me laugh. "And what do *you* want?"

Puck stared at me, pain flashing in his green eyes. "I swore I'd never be in another relationship."

"Another?" My voice cracked as I spoke the word, jealousy flooding me. It wasn't fair. I knew we all had pasts, even if mine was nothing but a blip. It was natural for wolves to seek out sexual touch. But something about how Puck spoke the words told me this was different.

He shifted, his gaze moving away from me and toward the windows. He stared out at the forest, no words coming for a moment. "My family comes from a royal line in Britain."

I blinked a few times. "Like you're the prince of England?"

Puck chuckled, but there was no humor in it. "Not those royals. Wolf royalty. My father runs the oldest pack in the United Kingdom. Quite a lot of power and wealth comes with that."

I'd bet. My father had become a less prestigious sort of

royal—a bayou royal. One who'd taken his power and riches by force. But it was a legacy all the same.

"I am his eldest son," Puck went on. "The next in line to the throne."

My fingers curved around the countertop's edge, holding on for dear life. "That has to come with a lot of pressure."

Puck kept staring at the trees like they held all the answers he needed. "It's funny. I didn't feel that growing up. My world was just...easy. I didn't think about what my future held until I turned thirteen and my father started training me."

My stomach sank as I remembered the sort of training my father took his wolves through, the kind he put me through.

Puck's gaze flicked to me for a moment. "Nothing horrible. Just the usual fare. Hand-to-hand. Weapons. Battle strategy. We spent a lot of time together. I didn't notice that it changed how my siblings looked at me."

"You have brothers and sisters?" I asked. I'd often longed for a sibling, wishing so desperately for someone to weather the storm with.

Puck nodded, true grief settling in his features. "One of each. But my younger brother wasn't pleased that I was to take on the role of alpha."

I sucked in a breath so sharp it stabbed. Power struggles in packs were far from unheard of, but when it came within families, there was an extra dose of agony. "Did he challenge you?"

Puck scoffed. "No. He knew he would lose. So, he made a grab for power another way."

My stomach twisted, but still I asked, "How?"

"When I was twenty-four, and he was twenty-two, a friend of Father's came to stay with us with his family. He had a daughter. We knew she was a potential for us both the moment we met her."

I bit the inside of my cheek as jealousy flared again. A potential mate. Someone Puck could've chosen to spend the rest of his very long supernatural life with and have pups with.

"Alice seemed taken with us both, interested in us both. I told Theo maybe this was our chance. To have a bond between the three of us. To rule together."

The twisting in my belly turned to a sick, foreboding feeling. "What happened?" I whispered.

A muscle in Puck's jaw began to flutter. "He agreed. I should've seen that he did it far too readily. We both began to spend time with Alice. Apart. Together. But I should've seen that he sought her out more than I did."

Puck's throat worked as he swallowed. "One night, she came to my room with wine. Poured us both a glass. I didn't notice the feeling of being out of it until it was too late. Until Theo showed up and demanded a challenge right then."

"She drugged you?" I snapped. Weakening someone before a challenge was the lowest of the low.

Puck jerked his head in a nod. "I had no choice but to accept. My mother wept and begged Theo to recant, but he wouldn't. I had no choice but to fight him."

"And you won," I surmised.

Puck's green gaze had no life in it now. "I killed him. I killed my brother. Because he refused to submit. And he knew that he'd never get the throne, the alpha position, so it was the only way to defeat me. And he did. I left Britain. Left the pack. My sister will lead them now. She's smarter than the rest of us anyway."

"You don't see your family?"

"No," he croaked. "Too many demons there."

"And Alice?" I spat her name like the vile disease she was.

Puck shrugged. "Left with her family, I'm sure to manipulate some other poor sap."

Understanding swept over me, pain rushing in along with it. "And you never wanted to go down the mate road again."

"No. I swore never again."

I stared at Puck, not moving from my spot. "Do you think I'm like her?"

The pain in his eyes intensified. "I know you're not. But that doesn't mean you don't have the power to hurt me—in a million different ways."

I moved then, crossing to him. I wanted to touch him so badly, but I knew I didn't have that right, not yet. Because the moment I touched Puck, the bond would strengthen, bringing us closer together. Instead, I put all the feelings I had into my words.

"And you could hurt me in a million different ways. We will hurt each other. That's life. But we will also do whatever it takes to make it right. And I *promise* I will never intentionally cause you pain. I will never try to steal your happiness."

Puck searched my eyes, emotion swimming in his. "Wren."

My name on his lips was like a caress as he moved closer. His head bent, his mouth just a breath away from mine.

"I wouldn't do that, brother." Ender's voice was colder than I had ever heard it. "Unless you want a snake in your bed."

I whirled around, confusion and hurt bleeding into my expression.

He glared at me, those amber eyes flashing gold. But not a gold of attraction or warmth. It was rage.

"What the hell are you going on about, End?" Puck demanded. "You need to stop with this vendetta against her."

"Do I?" Ender sneered, but his eyes never left mine. "Because I just got a call from a contact. And they know exactly who Wren is. The bastard daughter of Bastian Boudreaux. The alpha of the Red River pack."

CHAPTER FORTY-NINE

Wren

I FELT THE BLOOD DRAIN FROM MY HEAD, ONLY IT DIDN'T STOP there. It kept going until I was lightheaded and stumbling back into the kitchen island.

My mind spun, tripping over a million different thoughts as it did. I needed to know who Ender had spoken with and how they knew who I was. Icy dread slid through my veins. Did my father know where I was? Was he already coming for me?

"What's the matter?" Ender sneered. "Cat got your tongue?"

Puck shoved him. "Back off. You need proof that she's a part of that pack."

He said the word *pack* as if it were a curse. And it was. Having Red River blood running through my veins was a punishment no one deserved. But even worse was having Bastian Boudreaux's blood there, knowing that a man as evil as him was part of my fundamental makeup.

Just the reminder had acid sloshing through my stomach,

nausea quick on its heels. Memories slammed into me. All his *punishments* in an effort to make me strong.

"Fucking look at her," Ender demanded. "She's his."

"I'm not," I croaked. I finally forced my gaze up to take in Brix, King, and Locke, who'd spilled in behind Ender. They'd moved so silently I hadn't even heard them.

"Liar," Ender snarled, lifting his phone and shoving it into my face.

There was a photo on the screen. One from years ago. I was probably thirteen or so at the time, standing next to Bastian and his top enforcers, my arms wrapped around myself. I remembered the day. Another pack had come for a meeting, and Bastian had trotted me out for the party like he always did. The only problem was that he'd beaten me so badly the night before it had been painful to move.

Kingston looked from the phone to me and back again. "Tell me it isn't true. Tell me you're not the daughter of the man who stole my sister from me. Who turned her life into a living hell."

A whole new wave of nausea slid through me as pieces started to fall into place. A pack who kidnapped women and girls and sold them. I knew my father had been involved in illegal dealings, but I'd been far from being in his trusted circle. I hadn't known he'd gone *that* dark.

But I shouldn't be surprised.

My mouth felt like it was full of sand, but I forced myself to speak. "I'm not his daughter by choice."

Ender curled his upper lip, letting out a growl as he stalked toward me. "We're not falling for your innocent act. Not anymore."

Locke moved then, stepping between us and shoving Ender back a step. "Stop. You know she's been through hell."

"It's a fucking act," Ender snarled. "And you're falling for it."

Ender's anger was like fiery claws raking against my shields, sending countless tiny ice picks through my skull.

"No, you aren't seeing the truth because you're so caught up in your vendetta," Locke gritted out.

Ender's chest rose and fell in ragged pants as fur rippled over his forearms. "My vendetta? You mean the fact that I want revenge on the pack who slayed mine without any honor. Just to steal what we had. The pack that killed my entire family? Brix's family? Who almost killed Brix himself?"

Black spots danced in front of my vision—the only warning I had that I wasn't breathing. I forced myself to inhale, to take in the oxygen, even though I didn't want it. Didn't deserve it. I knew my father led raiding parties. He was hungry for riches and territory. Greedy.

Bastian would use every trick in the book to get what he wanted. There were no challenges. There were only the most ruthless tactics. He didn't care that he tore families apart and traumatized the survivors for the rest of their days.

I just didn't realize he'd done that to men I cared so deeply about. My gaze lifted, finding Kingston's locked on me. There was so much pain in those light-blue eyes. Total and complete agony. But there was also something else. He was looking at me like I was a complete stranger. As if he'd never laid eyes on me before.

It was like a dagger had been plunged into my chest. He might as well have rejected our mating bond right then and there. A cramping sensation took root in my stomach, waves of excruciating pain sloshing through me as I sought out Brix.

He stood the farthest away from me, back at the entryway to the kitchen. But his blue-green eyes had gone completely dead. There was no emotion in him at all. It was as if *I* was nothing to him.

A soft whimper left my lips, one I tried to swallow but couldn't. Ender's gaze shot instantly to me. "Don't you fucking dare. You don't get to keep this act up. You don't get to learn our secrets and report back to *Daddy*."

Bile surged up my throat, but I forced myself to straighten

and lift my chin. "He is not my father. He contributed to my DNA and nothing more."

Ender bared his teeth at me, trying to go around Locke, but Puck moved in to block him. The growl that left Ender's throat was one of pure rage. "You'd take her back after everything I've told you?"

"She's our mate," Puck stated with finality, his green eyes glinting with a hardness I'd never seen before.

"Your mate?" Ender spat. "I never thought *you* would fall for the con of a woman again."

The room went eerily silent. After everything Puck had shared with me, I knew why. That blow was too vicious, too brutal, especially between brothers. Puck's eyes swirled with rage as he gritted his teeth. "I'll let you have that *one* because of your wounds and losses. But only that one. Speak to me or Wren that way again, and I'll do more than break your nose."

Locke turned to me, reaching out as if to take my hand, but I skirted away. If he touched me now, it would break me. It would be the physical manifestation of everything I was losing. Everything that had made me feel whole for the first time in my life, only to be ripped out from under me.

Pain flashed in Locke's gray eyes, but there was also empathy. "Go to your room. Stay there. I'll come find you after we're done."

My heart clenched. He was still trying to protect me in his very Locke way. He didn't want me to hear Ender's cruel words or see the rejection in King's and Brix's gazes.

I moved quickly, slipping out the back entrance of the kitchen toward my room. Only I wouldn't stay there. There was only one thing I could do now.

Run.

CHAPTER FIFTY

Locke

I could feel Wren's pain reaching out to me like a living, breathing thing. Tendrils of it scraped against my skin, but more than that, I saw the life in her eyes fading. The vitality and fieriness drained with each second until she darted from the kitchen.

I watched her go. Waited for a count of five until I knew she'd had time to disappear behind her bedroom door, and then I whirled on Ender. My fist connected with his nose in a satisfying blow.

Fighting wasn't something I enjoyed the way my pack mates and brothers did. But in this case, I was willing to do whatever was necessary to protect Wren.

Ender's shock at my attack was short-lived. He answered with a blow to my ribs that forced all the air from my lungs and possibly cracked a bone or two.

I didn't give a damn. My fist connected with his jaw in an

answering uppercut that had his head jerking back with a satisfying snap.

Ender sent a roundhouse kick in my direction, but I ducked beneath it, sweeping his leg out from under him. He crashed into the kitchen table, fury on his face as he righted himself. "What the fuck is wrong with you?"

Kingston moved then, finally taking on a little of the alpha role he should've stepped into the moment Ender began railing against Wren. "Enough." His voice carried weight and fatigue in that single word. But he put a hand on Ender's chest to keep him from charging forward.

"Shouldn't you be telling *him* that? He's the one protecting that traitorous bitch," Ender snapped.

There were answering growls in the room from me, Puck, and even Brix.

Ender's jaw went slack. "You can't honestly tell me you're still falling for her shit."

"She's our mate," Brix gritted out.

"So fucking what?" Ender shot back.

"You can't fake that," Puck said quietly.

"Some sort of spell," Ender suggested.

I glared in his direction. "I've never heard of that kind of magic. Ever."

Though it wouldn't have mattered if I had. I knew that what I felt for Wren was real. The bond was real. She made me feel more at peace and seen than anyone ever had. She'd also been through hell. One that no one deserved—but especially her.

Ender scowled at me. "You might be a tech genius, but you don't know every piece of magic that exists."

"But I know Wren. Probably better than any of you do because I shut up and listen," I growled.

They all turned to me then. Even Brix's eyes widened a fraction as the shock hit them all.

"I've put the pieces together. She's running. Running from

someone who *hurt* her. Someone who left her body riddled with scars and terrified of the dark. Do you know what she said when the power went out? '*They hurt me in the dark.*'"

Those words had haunted me ever since. Replayed in my mind in an agonizing loop. I scanned the faces of the men in the room, males who were Wren's mates, my brothers. "She has been terrorized, touch-starved, and so much worse. And the three of you just wounded her worse than any of that by believing a bunch of bullshit lies."

Anger coursed through me. No, fury. Because I didn't have a clue how we'd undo the damage done over the past five minutes—if we even could. But I knew one thing for certain. If Wren decided she needed to leave, I was going with her.

I wasn't sure I'd ever be able to forgive Ender, or Kingston for that matter. I trusted our alpha to be smarter than this, more reasonable.

The color drained from King's face. "Fucking hell."

"Exactly," I snarled. "You're better than this."

Pain swept through his expression. "I know I am. I just—all I could think about was Natasha and what she'd been through. And knowing that Wren came from him…"

"Not by choice. She has been terrorized by the same man you three have. But it's so much worse because he was supposed to love her." I met each of their eyes, trying to punctuate my point.

Ender simply scoffed. "If you're still falling for her bullshit, you're stupider than I ever could've imagined," he spat as he stalked out of the kitchen. The door slammed a second later, and after a few more, thunder rolled.

It was fitting that a storm hit at a moment like this. I just hoped the power held this time. Lightning flashed, illuminating the kitchen. No one else had moved. We all stood there silently, thinking about the damage we'd wrought. None of us was innocent. Not even me.

Because I should've stopped Ender weeks ago. I should've

gone to King and forced him to make End leave until he was ready to come to terms with the fact that he had a true mate. But it was too late now. He'd inflicted the sort of damage that couldn't be undone.

Brix scrubbed a hand over his face and then raked his fingers down his neck, leaving red marks amid the ink. "She grew up with pure evil."

"She did," I said quietly.

I couldn't imagine what that had been like. All the ways she'd been hurt.

"What do you think happened to her mom?" Puck whispered.

More pain flooded Kingston's face. "I don't know, but I doubt it was good."

"We need to find out from Ender who his contact is. If Wren's been running from Bastian, this may have exposed her." Just saying the words out loud turned my stomach.

"He. Doesn't. Get. Her," Brix growled. "She won't be hurt. Never again."

That was a vow I could live by. Wren had endured too much pain in her life. And she'd only been caused more tonight. I wouldn't allow that to continue.

Kingston turned to me. "You still have eyes on them, right?"

"As much as I can. But you know Red River keeps their movements locked up tight." I'd been trying for a way in, but they must've had a hacker in the pack. Someone made their systems almost impenetrable.

"We keep our eyes peeled and ears to the ground. I want us to keep a lookout for any unfamiliar faces around town. Wren's eyes and scars make her unique. It's not like she can disguise who she is," Kingston said.

Puck shook his head. "We keep her in the compound for now. No work for a while."

"Good luck with that," I muttered.

One corner of King's mouth kicked up. "Locke has a point."

"We can make a plan later. Right now, we need to be there

for her. And you fuckers need to apologize," I ground out, already heading toward the back hall.

I heard footsteps behind me and knew my brothers were following, but I could only think about Wren. Her door was shut, that single visual like an invisible fist grinding against my sternum. I lifted my hand and knocked three times. There was no answer.

I wasn't shocked by the lack of response, but it still burned. "Wren?" I called. "It's me."

Still no answer.

Puck muttered a curse. "I'm going to kill Ender."

I tried the doorknob. It was unlocked, so I slowly opened the door and stepped inside. Everything was quiet except for the pounding rain against the windows and roof. Scanning the space, I moved deeper into the room. No sign of Wren.

My heart picked up speed as I checked the closet and bathroom. Then I hurried back out to the bedroom, true panic setting in. "She's gone."

CHAPTER FIFTY-ONE

Wren

RAIN POUNDED DOWN, MAKING MY HAIR STICK TO MY face, and my clothes cling to my body. I shivered, the water making the air seem at least ten degrees colder as the darkness encroached. I picked up my pace, jogging toward the two-lane road that led into town.

I'd never been more grateful for the flashes of lightning that occasionally pierced the sky. I held on to those flickers of light, telling myself over and over that I wasn't in the dark because another flash was coming. But those reassurances did nothing for the pain in my heart.

It intensified with each step I took away from the mansion nestled in the woods. I knew it was the bond crying out, telling me to go back. Only I couldn't. It was the only way I could keep myself and the men I cared about safe.

Men I cared about even amid their rejection. Men I was falling for. My tears mixed with the rain as they slid down my face and dripped off my chin.

Headlights flashed in the night, and I stepped deeper into the trees. I couldn't risk anyone spotting me. I needed to make it to Arcane, my hidey-hole of identities and cash, and my beater of a car. Then, I had to run.

I watched as the SUV I knew belonged to Puck drove slowly by. They were searching for me, and the pain in my chest only intensified at that knowledge.

Leaving would do one thing: It would tell them all that Ender was right. That I was only out for myself and my father.

It didn't matter that it was a lie. It was a lie that would save us all.

Because if my father found out I had true mates, he'd only want one thing.

To slaughter them all.

Bastian wasn't someone who took pleasure in his daughter's happiness. He only wanted my pain. Because he considered me weaker than him. Less than.

My survival alone made him look weak. Because I'd escaped his circle of evil, his pack that lived on blood and pain.

I shuddered against the cold and memories, then picked up my pace again. Running would help keep me warm. My duffel slammed against my back with each step, but I welcomed the discomfort. I hoped it would distract me from the agony in my chest.

It didn't. The pain of leaving the guys was too great.

More tears came as memories swept through me. The way Locke touched me as much as possible, never wanting me to feel alone. The meals Puck prepared, always wanting me to be well fed. How Kingston trained me, wanting me to be ready for whatever came my way. And how Brix let me touch him when he couldn't bear for anyone else to even be close.

I didn't let myself think about Ender. Not even the one stolen afternoon we'd shared where he taught me how to shoot a bow and arrow. Because his hatred wasn't something that could be undone.

Not that it mattered. I should've known I'd never be able to keep the luxury of connection. Not if I wanted to stay alive.

By the time I reached town, my teeth were chattering, and every last inch of me was drenched. The lightning had eased, but the rain kept coming. Maybe that was for the best. I needed the cover of darkness now.

I reminded myself of that over and over. Darkness was my friend. It was keeping me safe, hidden from prying eyes.

I slipped between a fly-fishing shop and Arcane, moving toward the back of the building. I stilled when I heard voices. Puck and Kingston.

"She's not anywhere in there," Puck called. "Not the bar, the office, or the apartment."

Kingston cursed, and I inched forward, needing one more look at them before I left forever. My heart ached as I watched them in the rain. King raked a hand through his dark hair, his pale-blue eyes a little wild. "Come on," he yelled. "Let's check the gym. Maybe she went there."

I waited as they climbed into the SUV and headed for Crescent Kingdom. I ran for Arcane's back entrance when I saw them disappear inside. Sliding my key into the lock, I quickly opened the door and slipped through the opening.

Running up the stairs, I unlocked my apartment door and dashed in. I'd need to wait until the guys left the gym before I made a run for it. And I'd have to ditch my car as soon as I made it to Denver. I couldn't have them tracking me that way.

I'd head north to Montana, southwest to Arizona, or maybe go all the way northeast to Maine. Those decisions could come with time. What mattered now was getting the hell out of Crescent Creek while I still could.

I dropped to my knees, the action jarring my spine as I opened my secret hiding spot. I shoved everything into my duffel, then put the floorboard back. Since I had a few minutes to spare, I emptied the contents of my closet into another bag and slung it over my shoulder.

Moving to the window facing the gym, I peered out. The SUV was gone. A pang struck my heart, but I shoved the feeling down.

Alive. I had to stay alive. That was what mattered. My life and theirs. And this was the only way.

Gripping my keys tighter, I headed back to the stairs and jogged down to the back door. I waited for a moment and then scanned the back parking lot. There were no signs of movement, so I slipped out again.

I beeped the locks on my vehicle and quickly shoved my bags into the back seat. That's when I felt it. The slight shift in the air. A scent that wasn't familiar.

But it was too late.

A hand fisted my hair as a face pressed in next to mine. "Lookie what I found. A Diablos bitch. I think she might send a good message."

I didn't have a chance to move or fight because, before I did, a blade jabbed into my ribs. It was so fast and hard I thought it was just a punch at first. Only the burning pain and the way all my strength fled as I crumpled to the cement told me it was more.

Dark figures swam in the rain above me. And then the darkness swallowed me whole.

ALSO BY TESSA HALE

Wolves of Crescent Creek

Crescent Kingdom

Eclipsed Empire

Rising Reign

The Dragons of Ember Hollow

Twilight of Embers

Midnight of Ashes

Dawn of Flames

Supernaturals of Castle Academy

Legacy of Shadows

Anchor of Secrets

Destiny of Ashes

Royals of Kingwood Academy

The Lost Elemental

The Last Aether

The Queen of Quintessence

The Shifting Fate Series

Spark of Fate

Mark of Stars

Bond of Destiny

CONNECT WITH TESSA

You can find Tessa at various places on the internet.
These are her favorites…

Website
www.tessahale.com

Newsletter
tessahale.com/newsletter

Facebook Page
bit.ly/TessaHaleFB

Facebook Reader Group
bit.ly/TessaHaleBookHangout

Instagram
instagram.com/tessahalewrites

Goodreads
bit.ly/TessaHaleGR

BookBub
bookbub.com/authors/tessa-hale

Amazon
bit.ly/TessaHaleAmazon

ABOUT TESSA HALE

Author of love stories with magic, usually with more than one love interest. Constant daydreamer.